Bled Dry

Abdelilah Hamdouchi

hoopoe

AN IMPRINT OF AUC PRESS

First published in 2017 by
Hoopoe
113 Sharia Kasr el Aini, Cairo, Egypt
420 Fifth Avenue, New York, 10018
www.hoopoefiction.com

Hoopoe is an imprint of the American University in Cairo Press
www.aucpress.com

Exclusive distribution outside Egypt and North America by I.B.Tauris & Co Ltd.,
6 Salem Road, London, W4 2BU

Dar el Kutub No. 26266/16
ISBN 978 977 416 848 2

Dar el Kutub Cataloging-in-Publication Data

Hamdouchi, Abdelilah
        Bled Dry / Abdelilah Hamdouchi.—Cairo: The American University in
    Cairo Press, 2017.
        p. cm.
        ISBN 978 977 416 848 2
        1. Murder—Morocco—Casablanca—Fiction
        2. Police—Morocco—Casablanca—Fiction
        3. Arabic Fiction
        892.73

1 2 3 4 5   21 20 19 18 17

Designed by Adam el-Sehemy
Printed in the United States of America

1

NEZHA WASN'T YET TWENTY YEARS old, but she looked like a prostitute on the verge of early retirement. Layer after layer of makeup had transformed the softness and innocence of her face, giving her a severe pallor. Wrinkles from frequent all-nighters were carved deeply into her features. She had difficulty erasing the blue hue of her lips caused by all the smoking, and the whiteness of her teeth had given way to a strange yellowish color.

She sauntered down the sidewalk carrying her small handbag, and without a bra her breasts almost spilled out of her shirt. Her high heels caused her to wobble and walk crookedly. She was intentionally giving the impression that she was an easy catch. She stirred up the passing drivers so much that one car nearly hit another. An intoxicated driver slowed to cruise alongside her with his head out the window, telling her about the wild night he'd have in store for her. Even though Nezha tried to give the impression that she was enjoying all this attention, deep down she shuddered with fear as she walked alone down the sidewalk of a dangerous street that was empty of other pedestrians at this late hour.

She was, in fact, carrying out the terms of a pact she had agreed to in order to satisfy the vanity of an older man, who got off on watching this.

Hamadi pulled up in his Mercedes. He gave a subtle signal and she hurried toward him. She spoke to him, leaning her elbows on the base of the car's open window, and meanwhile thrusting out her ass as far as possible. Her movements were overly provocative. Inebriated drivers drooled, and not a single one protested that the Mercedes was blocking the street—until she got in.

Hamadi let out a triumphant laugh and turned toward Nezha, looking first at her makeup-caked face and then lowering his gaze to her bare thighs. He continued his boisterous and repulsive cackle while repeating all sorts of obscenities about how he wanted to force himself on top of her. She fired back with even more obscene language, detailing how she wanted to be pounded by him.

The dirty talk was all part of the game, but when Hamadi used this language it seemed out of place. He was close to sixty years old. His features projected a stern and serious disposition, accentuated by his thick black glasses. He was a shrewd banker who had climbed the rungs of the ladder and was now bank manager. A bruise—commonly adorning the foreheads of those who prayed frequently—was his stamp of piety. His depravities with a girl the age of his younger daughter did not suit him. Instead, they made him an object of scorn, even in Nezha's eyes. She thought he was revolting, but nonetheless, she tried her best to provide him with some lewd new joke.

They had met when the bank refused to cash her check for a paltry sum. The check was for ninety dirhams, and the lowest amount the bank would cash was one hundred. A customer had given her the check after a blowjob in his car, while he was driving, that had barely lasted a minute. The bank teller knew the check would bounce, but Nezha complained about him anyway, as if he were the person responsible for cheating her. The teller transferred her to the manager, Hamadi. She had hoped that he would treat her with the respect and affection of the father she had lost, but since that day she became Hamadi's companion for his "day of depravity," always the first Saturday of each month.

The moment the parking attendant saw the Mercedes pull up, he found them a spot reserved for well-known patrons. Nezha got out of the car and waited for Hamadi to lock the door. Hamadi was of average height, and this evening he was dressed casually, looking like someone who had just changed out of his work clothes. He hid the wrinkles on his neck behind a colorful scarf, which gave him an effeminate look. As soon as he saw the bouncer Farqash he rushed to greet him, but Farqash fixed his bone-chilling gaze on Nezha as they entered. Farqash twitched his head threateningly in her direction, indicating that serious punishment was in store.

The bar La Falaise was really a stop-off before heading out to the clubs, which didn't open their doors until after midnight. The bar was located downtown, close to the famous café La Choppe. It had an unlit entrance on an alley-way that led to a side street, where there was a secret door to the bar that only the employees knew about. It was swarming with beautiful young girls, most of whom were sitting with old men. The unaccompanied women sat smoking, legs crossed, waiting for a customer who was looking for a good time. The criteria for admitting women to La Falaise were very strict and centered foremost on beauty and youth, and then on the amount of money each girl could pay the hideous Farqash.

Farqash was absolutely repulsive: he had a huge bald head, wide-set eyes, and a flat nose. His build was sturdy, and he always seemed ready for a fight. He was known for all manner of depravities: he was a pimp, a middleman, a crook, and a police informant. He had been imprisoned multiple times, and it was there—the rumor went—that he had begun dealing cocaine. The drug infested Casablanca, coming from Ceuta, the Spanish enclave in the north, where it was exchanged for hash.

This was the man who ruled over La Falaise. Every girl gave him a percentage of what she made from her customers, and had to pay even if she made nothing that night. She even had to pay for her own cigarettes and drinks. When leaving, she had to place a tip in the palm of his hand.

Farqash and Nezha had history together. Not long ago she had been his favorite— his spoiled lover, preferred over all the other women at the bar. But he had taken to another girl who had recently entered the scene, and since then he had begun treating Nezha like garbage. Just a month ago he demanded that she pay him, like everyone else. He'd had his fill and was tired of her. Nezha kept putting off paying him, but yesterday he had given her one final deferment, and time was up tonight.

The law of La Falaise was firm: each girl was required to encourage her client to consume a specific amount of alcohol before leaving the bar. In addition, she was required to arrange their future rendezvous at La Falaise. If the girl wanted to continue working there, she had to follow these rules. If she ended up stealing customers away by suggesting a different meeting place, she would be kicked out of the bar and face one of two options: either Farqash would smash her face in himself, or he would instruct one of the many young street kids waiting in the alley outside to permanently disfigure her with a razor blade, so that no man would want anything to do with her ever again.

Farqash's new darling was really young. She had been plucked by one of the female scouts at the courtroom doors, moments after the judge ruled for divorce. This scout then sold her to Farqash for five hundred dirhams. In less than a week, Farqash had trained her to obey him and to master her new trade. As she was blessed with a winning combination—a tall and slender figure, a huge bosom, and an alluring face— he made her a barmaid. He also gave her a new name, Warda, instead of her Bedouin name, Hada. Despite having worked at La Falaise for over a month now, she hadn't quite managed to give up her comical Bedouin habits, which seemed to really arouse the customers.

Warda leaned down to give Nezha a kiss on each cheek, and then gave Hamadi an enthusiastic kiss just beside his mouth, angering Nezha. This uncouth Bedouin girl had taken her place with Farqash and now she was attempting to steal Nezha's generous once-a-month customer! Warda brought them to their usual table in the corner and bowed respectfully. A minute later she returned with a cold beer, some snacks, and a pack of Marlboros for Nezha.

The bar was packed and full of commotion, contrary to what it looked like from the exterior. The floor was upholstered in dark-red moquette and the round tables were surrounded by chairs that had embroidered covers. The walls were covered with massive drapes, giving the impression that there were windows even though there weren't any. The bar counter in the center of the room was dimly lit with red lights that hung from the ceiling, like an island detached from the rest of the place. La Falaise's esteemed patrons were accompanied by beautiful half-naked girls. The regulars stood near the bar, an intimate meeting point where a newcomer would feel out of place and probably wouldn't last very long.

Saturday night was different from other nights, as a band took over the small stage and played popular songs, replacing the original lyrics with comical and vulgar insertions.

Hamadi was returning to his senses, as the effects of the whiskey he had consumed before meeting up with Nezha wore off. He averted his eyes from her as though he'd forgotten her altogether. She knew this state all too well. The sobriety affected him temporarily until the alcohol in the beer was able to snap him out of it again. She took advantage of this opportunity to head to the bathroom. As soon as she disappeared into the drunken crowd, Farqash grabbed her by the neck and dragged her into a dark corner of the bar. He wrapped his arms around her as if choking her—intent on squeezing her so hard she couldn't breathe.

"My money! Where is my money?"

She couldn't speak, as she was nearly suffocating. He loosened his hold just a bit, so she was able to open her mouth.

"Tomorrow, Farqash," she said, her voice trembling. "Tomorrow you'll get it all."

"If you don't give me my money tomorrow, I will slaughter you. I'll decapitate you."

He scowled at her and pressed hard on her cheeks. Then he rammed his tongue deep into her throat and spat in her mouth. She was disgusted by him and rushed to the sink to vomit.

Nezha returned and found that Hamadi had consumed two beers, one after the other, in record time. She sat in front of him. The clamor and dim lighting, not to mention her skill in hiding her feelings, meant he didn't notice the anger written on her face. Insults and abuse didn't affect her for more than a few passing moments. She had become used to all kinds of curses, humiliations, and degradations. What she really feared was a punch knocking out some teeth, a razor disfiguring her face, or gang rape. Except for those scenarios, nothing else mattered much. She had learned that returning home safely at the end of the night was the best that girls like her could hope for.

She let out a high-pitched squeal when Hamadi reached under the table and caressed her thighs, pushing his fingers between them. She giggled and drew his hand even closer, acting as if she enjoyed his fondling. This was exactly what Hamadi loved about her: this brazenness that a man couldn't find with his wife. A prostitute searches for pleasure and embraces it.

He pulled off his scarf, revealing his ruddy, wrinkled neck with flabby layers of skin. He pulled Nezha close and whipped the scarf around her ass. She began to dance for him alone in their dark corner to the lyrics "What will he do? They brought him love at three in the morning." The singer switched the word *love* in the song to a dirty word for sex. Hamadi couldn't resist this: Nezha writhing in front of him above his lap, leaning over him so her hair touched him. He smacked her on the ass and let out a loud bellow. This was the declaration that the alcohol was taking over, and that the real excitement had just begun.

The evening in Casablanca doesn't really begin until after midnight, and after midnight anything goes. Where would Hamadi decide to end their evening? They left La Falaise after one in the morning. In the car, Nezha tried to be more seductive, caressing his temple with her palm and distracting him as he drove.

"Where are you taking me, Daddy?" she said flirtatiously, as she blew cigarette smoke in his face.

He looked her over with a lecherous smile and grabbed her chest. "Hopefully to hell!" he responded.

The car took off into the street and Nezha knew that they weren't heading toward Ain Diab, as she had hoped. Ain Diab was full of nightclubs frequented by Gulfies, strip clubs blaring pop music patronized by wealthy businessmen and power brokers, and whorehouses that stayed open into the wee hours of the morning with raucous parties that became the talk of the town the next day. Rather, he would force her to take a nauseating trip around the streets that occupied the most beautiful stretches of the city in the daytime, but that by night became exhibition grounds for the sale of sex.

The car had just pulled into the first street when two young men emerged from behind the trees, exposing their erect penises to the johns, who slowed their pace. An adolescent boy with a thin moustache approached their car, showing off his goods, letting it be known that he would have sex with men or women, no problem. Then another approached from Hamadi's side. The car had barely passed the two men who had emerged from the trees when a row of transvestites emerged in their tight women's clothing, hair cut like girls', and their faces smeared heavily with makeup. They were sauntering around flirtatiously, winking at passersby, snapping their chewing gum, and blowing air kisses to drivers.

Only a few steps away from the gays and transvestites were the "open-air" prostitutes, who would have sex in that very spot for a small sum—no more than fifty dirhams. You would just head into the wooded area nearby, take off your pants, and finish off the job on all fours, like a wild dog, without a condom or any other protection. If one of the prostitutes asked you to wear a condom, that usually meant she had HIV. They stood there, legs swollen from fatigue, only a few feet separating one from the other, while stoned young men stood by to watch over them and take a cut of the profits. This type of prostitute was at the bottom of the barrel. Most of them were over forty and were either divorced or widowed, but still had families to support. If no one chose them that evening and the night passed without any business, they would transition to begging at daybreak. Or they would give a quick blowjob in an alley for twenty dirhams.

This was the sex market that began every night at midnight and lasted until daybreak. Competition intensified on the first Saturday of the month, when men's pockets were flush with their wages. Hamadi loved taking an excursion through this dissolute marketplace. It really turned him on. But he cut the tour short and their trip abruptly ended at Hotel Scheherazade, crushing Nezha's hopes of heading to one of the nightclubs in Ain Diab.

From the outside, Hotel Scheherazade seemed like a respectable establishment, but it was really a dressed-up brothel. It was located on a narrow street downtown, surrounded by bars and cafés. However, it was rare that a tourist would stay there, since the dimly lit sign bearing the hotel's name was barely visible. The girls who hung around the neighborhood were hunting for customers they could bring back to the hotel. The proprietor was a reformed drug dealer who was able to launder money through the hotel. He enjoyed police protection and had made shady deals with the authorities so they would turn a blind eye. After all, it was illegal for a couple to share a hotel room without providing their marriage license.

The big problem for men like Hamadi, who relished their rare nights out on the town, was where to hide away with their girls. Most of the hotel's repeat clientele were serial adulterers, addicted to cheating on their wives. The bulk of them were respected officials, teachers, and other government employees. The way things worked at the hotel was that a customer paid for two rooms: one for himself, and a separate one for the girl with him. Of course, once inside, they met up in the same room. Added to the room charge was a fixed price for "special patrons"—an extra charge so the police would turn a blind eye.

Nezha was one of the familiar faces at the hotel. When she approached the reception with Hamadi—both of them stumbling drunkenly—the doorman quickly greeted them, knowing a generous tip awaited him. Though he was yawning at this late hour, he cheerfully opened the door. There wasn't really any furniture in the seedy lobby, just a single tattered couch that the doorman slept on, and a chair with a broken leg that looked completely uninviting to sit on. It was clear that the lobby was not designed to welcome any sort of normal guest.

As they approached, the concierge tossed his newspaper aside and pretended to be serious. "Is this man with you?" he asked Nezha, as if he'd never met her.

Nezha glanced at herself in the broken mirror on the wall and fixed her short skirt. "I don't know him. I've never seen him before," she replied.

She lit a cigarette and blew smoke in the concierge's face. He was young, with stern features. He was overdoing his questioning, as if his job, and the hotel, were respectable. He had run through the formalities of this check-in procedure many a time, and being vigilant demanded that he treat all guests as if they were new arrivals. He placed one key in front of Nezha and a second in front of Hamadi. This part of the night always embarrassed Hamadi. Preferring not to say anything, Hamadi gave the concierge a conspiratorial smile, and then placed the money for the two rooms in front of him, along with an overly generous tip.

The room they shared was lit with a single dull lamp that belonged in a basement, not a hotel room. There was a sagging bed in the middle of the room that had clearly been hastily straightened out. A single long pillow without a cover was perched on the bed, on top of a stained bedsheet. There was no way that sheet was getting clean, no matter what laundry detergent was used. The bathroom emitted a strong smell of something in between bleach and urine. A filthy curtain covered a tightly locked window that looked like it hadn't been opened in years.

Nezha sat down on the edge of the slightly damp bed. As she stretched out on her back a cockroach shot out from under the bed and climbed the curtain. Nezha hitched her dress up higher to reveal her beautiful ivory thighs. Her soft white skin exuded the youthfulness of her tight twenty-year-old body. Quite the opposite of her face, ruined by all the smoking, late nights, alcohol, and makeup. Hamadi studied her for a while, attempting to dismiss whatever was troubling him. Something didn't feel right this time, and it was spoiling his mood. He looked at his watch. It was two thirty. He gazed at Nezha, but wasn't turned on at all. She sensed his boredom and began shifting around on the bed, posing in different erotic positions, copying what she had seen in pornos.

Nezha's antics didn't do much for Hamadi. What got him going was moaning coming from the bed in the room next door. There were shrieks, gasps, delirious laughter, and other sex noises. In a heartbeat he stripped off his clothes and lay back on the bed. That was really all he had to do, since Nezha was determined that tonight she would help him reach a new horizon of pleasure. She was hoping to fulfill his desires two-fold, in hopes that he would be more generous, so she could pay Farqash. Merely the thought of Farqash filled her with dread; she remembered his vile spit in the back of her throat. She refocused, trying to lose herself in lust with Hamadi. This customer could be her savior with his generosity.

She straddled him and began to dance above him, whipping him with her hair and driving him crazy. She started massaging his ruddy, flabby skin, and he moaned as she sucked him off. Every movement she made reflected her total absorption in the task, and Hamadi felt he was going to pass out from pleasure. They were naked on the bed as she embraced him, drew him in, licked him, and teased him with her tongue. She kissed him passionately all over his body, doing everything in her power to keep him erect. Hamadi's weakness was that his interest would wane halfway through.

She had slept with all types of men, and in the process had liberated herself from feelings of shame, disgust, or superiority. Nezha undertook her work with complete professionalism, and even took satisfaction in doing it well.

Hamadi was overwhelmed, and began moaning and speaking deliriously. Unable to process anything, he simply let out a shriek, like a calf being slaughtered.

Nezha lay beside him, still sweating. He turned toward her and began showering her with compliments. To his weary eyes she seemed so full of life. He was seized by an intense jealousy when he thought about her doing the same thing, with the same vigor, with other men. She lay there, thinking about opening up and telling him everything—divulging the details of her problems with Farqash. She thought about bringing up even more intimate things—her mother's illness and brother's unemployment—as a way to tug on his heartstrings, in hopes that he would be more generous with her than last time. But if she started along this path she knew he would withdraw from her, and retreat into a deep slumber.

She lit a cigarette and exhaled the smoke as she listened to the far-off moans, creaking beds, and other exclamations of love from the other rooms. She found consolation in taking deep drags from her cigarette and blowing out the smoke. This old man, after a long night, saw nothing but a cheap body he craved for an evening, and that was it.

For the first time ever she imagined her fingers sneaking toward his wallet, which was peeking out of the pocket of the pants tossed on the chair. If she found the cash to free her from her problems she would steal it. She hesitated, and just as she started to creep off the bed she heard the sounds of boots climbing the stairs. She heard knocking on one door after another and voices in the hallway yelled "Police! Police!" Had they come to arrest her just because she'd *thought* about stealing?

Nezha held her breath. Hamadi opened his eyes, his thoughts racing, and he began scanning the room. They both froze, still naked, waiting for what was to come.

There were two light knocks on the door, as if room service were making an inquiry.

"This is Detective Hanash. Open the door," said a calm voice.

Shaking, his legs barely able to support him, Hamadi hastily got dressed. He zipped up his fly, on the verge of collapsing.

2

DETECTIVE HANASH WAS IN HIS fifties, and only a few years from retirement. Everything about him suggested a man who had spent a lifetime interrogating criminals, studying murderers, and unraveling clues to crimes. This was how he got the nickname "Hanash," which meant "snake." His real name was Mohamed Bineesa. He would change character by "shedding his skin" and then "strike" his prey. Those who met Detective Hanash for the first time immediately got a sense of his strange personality, and those who had met him on multiple occasions tended to find him quite unpleasant. He was tall and slender, but had a smallish head that was always tilted toward his left shoulder. He had beady eyes without eyelashes that cast a confrontational expression. With a furrowed brow, he would stare sharply at his interlocutor with a suspicious and probing glare, as if he were searching for an accusation to pin on him. He had acquired this behavior from the excessive amount of time he spent with criminals. Even in his personal life he was incapable of relinquishing these mannerisms. He always seemed distracted and preoccupied by his thoughts. He never expressed interest in what others said. Nonetheless, everyone attested to his intelligence and total devotion to his work.

After so many years together, his wife, Naeema, had become a carbon copy of him—she was headstrong and extremely suspicious. Her demeanor never changed, no matter how much makeup she put on. She had dreamed of being blonde, but she was a brunette with darker skin. She had a deep, hoarse voice, and words seemed to rattle around in her throat. Despite these attributes, Hanash considered himself lucky. She was the ideal wife for someone in his profession.

In addition to being a skilled housewife, Naeema had learned a tremendous amount from her husband—in particular, his investigative techniques. She was aware of everything that transpired in the neighborhood; nothing got by her. Her speech was circuitous, and she would never reveal her true intentions. When chatting with someone her eyes would shift instinctively, as if any opinion she didn't share was dead wrong, or as if the speaker was lying. She considered even the most trifling family details crucial, and she had loyal informants—starting with the maid. She could thread together a scattered story from loose ends. She would trim any unnecessary details until she formed a crystal-clear picture. She would extract lively stories from her neighbors' chatter and gossip and then report them to her husband when he returned at night. He would feign interest to humor her, acting as if everything she told him was crucial to his own work. Sometimes he would even jot down something she said to make her feel like her intel was vital. She didn't really care if he believed her or considered her a gossip queen; what was crucial was that he didn't interrupt her, never appeared to tire of her, and showed surprise at the right moment. He would even ask about the sources of her information, and then charge her with pursuing her investigations further.

Naeema was an accomplished cook—her skill in the kitchen was unparalleled. She was always up early, rain or shine, to start her day in the kitchen. Listening to traditional music, she would prepare breakfast with finesse and concentration. As soon as the family left the house in the morning and the maid began cleaning and dusting, she would dive into preparations for the next meal with equal relish. She would pop in another CD, turning the volume all the way up, taking advantage of the empty house.

Of course, Hanash rarely returned for lunch, and so she would engage in some detective work of her own—covertly questioning one of his assistants in the hope of confirming if he would be home. If he wasn't, she would prepare a meal, even a traditional tagine dish, and pack it up like one of those prepared meals from a restaurant. Despite this, there was little intimacy in her relationship with her husband. It had been years since Hanash had demonstrated the type of passion they had previously shared. He used to take her by surprise in the bedroom even before he had time to take off his police uniform and disarm. In thinking about their passion-filled past, Naeema couldn't help but think how her current situation simply didn't compare.

Hanash had lost his desire for his wife and had been avoiding her for some time now—and she knew it. She chalked this up to his constant preoccupation with murderers, criminals, and other derelicts. The problem was, he was more distracted from her than ever before. Criminal activity had increased over the past years, due to rising unemployment, violence, terrorism, and access to the Internet, which helped in the globalization of criminality.

Outside of the bedroom, however, her married life was great. She lacked nothing. Her husband even gave her control over the family's financial matters, placing piles of cash in her care, never even counting it. He would give her unexpected gifts, though they were things that had been given to him. He never bought anything—everything he wanted was given to him for free—he just picked up the phone and ordered. He always had her back when she had disagreements with the kids, regardless of whether she was right or wrong. He only asked for one thing in exchange for all this—that she not cast so much as a speck of doubt on his relationships outside the home, which included not asking him about the women whom he greeted on the street, mentioned in passing, or whose names popped up on his phone.

Hanash's home was a villa from the French colonial period—a time when villas were luxurious, with high ceilings, spacious rooms, sweeping balconies, and lush gardens. As of late, high-rises had been creeping closer to this neighborhood on one side, and a single villa was now worth ten million dirhams, if not more. Hanash had taken notice of this trend, and with a bit of meddling here and there, he was successful in transferring the villa from governmental ownership to his own personal possession. A huge sum no doubt awaited him if he ever thought about selling.

Hanash and Naeema had a son and two daughters. Manar was twenty-five and couldn't exactly be described as beautiful or ugly. From her father she had inherited an unsettling smile, beady eyes, and olive skin. Manar hadn't completed her studies, and in place of going to university she got a certificate in hairdressing. She opened up a salon that her father was able to rent for her at an extremely reasonable price through his connections. He outfitted it with all the best equipment, and her clients took to calling her salon "The Commissioner's Daughter."

Tarek was the youngest in the family. He was in his second year of university, studying law. His aim was to pass the police academy exam after he got his law degree.

Atiqa, their second daughter, was the only sibling who had inherited her grandparents' good looks. She had men swooning over her and asking to marry her before she even turned twenty. Despite her father's urging, she did not complete her studies, but instead fell in love with the young man who became her husband. He was serious and handsome. He got a degree in accounting, and then went on to find a good job in the Marrakesh tax administration. Atiqa had been determined to marry him and refused to listen to opposing viewpoints. It had been impossible to dissuade her. So, in the end, her father gave in. He conceded to himself that the apple hadn't fallen too far from the tree when it came to Atiqa and his wife—both were content as housewives.

Before transferring to his current job in Casablanca, Hanash had completed an impressive stint in Tangier as the head of the criminal investigation unit focused on drug trafficking. It was a real golden age for Detective Hanash, during which he amassed both wealth and experience. His infallible police instincts led to his involvement in the Grand Campaign, which resulted in the imprisonment of some of the country's biggest hash barons, along with other crooks from the government's security apparatus. They included stubborn politicians and stingy businessmen, who were arrested either because they hadn't handed over their kickbacks or because their competitors wanted to take over their positions and business interests. Any charge of involvement in drug production or trafficking could land a suspect in prison for years.

The fame that Detective Hanash achieved in Tangier through his leading role in the Grand Campaign preceded him, to the present day. He became a national hero in combating drug trafficking. Of course, the campaign went down with the cooperation of certain higher-ups, who made millions from the hash industry in Tangier. They knew about the operation against the hash barons well in advance. In fact, they had prepared a blacklist for Hanash, which included the names of anyone who couldn't pay up, or who just needed to be eliminated.

This campaign followed on the heels of intense lobbying by European nations, which accused the Moroccan government of being lenient toward the drug organizations. Several reports had been published in the foreign press that labeled Morocco "Africa's Colombia" and singled out several prominent officials for accepting bribes and being involved with the international drug mafia. A few Spanish papers claimed that hash brought billions of euros to Morocco—more than all other foreign exports combined. The straw that broke the camel's back was an intense campaign by a Spanish lobby that aimed to pressure Morocco into reducing its fishing yield and agricultural exports in the European market. The government saw no other way to appease Spain than carrying out this campaign. Prior to the operation, necessary measures were taken to protect the fat cats. And it was none other than Detective Hanash—Tangier's top investigator at the time— who oversaw all these preparations.

Just a few weeks prior to the start of the campaign, Hanash submitted a list to his bosses that included the names of drug dealers who would take the fall, as well as the members of the security apparatus and businessmen connected to them, who would also be charged. After the well-publicized trials and delivery of the sentences—many for decades of imprisonment—the press declared Detective Hanash a hero, and he was quickly appointed head of criminal investigations in Casablanca.

Detective Hanash's big score in the Grand Campaign in Tangier, however, was his beloved mistress, Bushra al-Rifiya. Her husband Mohamed, nicknamed al-Sabliyuni meaning 'the Spaniard,' had been abducted by a gang that insisted that she not notify the police. She did the exact opposite, and called Detective Hanash.

When she entered his office that morning, he knew right away that she was the wife of either a high-caliber drug dealer or a shady businessman. She was clearly the type of woman who played with fire. Hanash couldn't get any words out at first, and he could feel his heart start to race. It was a warm morning, void of the easterly wind common in Tangier. Hanash was used to dealing with beautiful women, since the city swarmed with gorgeous women of the north who had Andalusian roots. But Bushra was something else altogether. She had a mesmerizing smile, an elegant nose seemingly carved from marble, and warm honey-colored eyes that you could never get enough of. He guessed that she was in her mid-thirties.

He extended his hand and asked her to have a seat.

What would bring a woman like this to the office of the drug cartels' number-one enemy?

"Yes, ma'am. What can I help you with?" he asked, trying his best to maintain an authoritative tone.

She stared at him with unexpected calm. "Are you . . . Detective Hanash?" she asked.

He looked around as if she were referring to someone else and then took a moment to scrutinize her. "My real name is Bineesa," he said finally, "but if you know who it was who first called me Hanash, I want to bring him to justice! And you? Who are you? And how did you get into my office?"

"I bribed the guard," she said casually, gesturing toward the door.

Hanash leaned back in his leather swivel chair, clasped his hands behind his neck, and looked at her carefully. He was starting to have serious doubts—was this a ruse? Her smile, self-assuredness, and calm were indicative of a woman who was used to all the chips falling in her favor. On top of that, her devastating beauty gave her a confidence he had never seen before. She was calm and collected, knowing in advance that she would always receive a warm welcome.

"May I have the pleasure of knowing with whom I'm speaking?"

"My name is Bushra al-Rifiya," she said, staring at him as if it were a test. "I was living with my husband in Spain, and we settled here in Tangier not too long ago."

Hanash smiled to himself even before she ended her sentence. This was what he had thought all along. He extended his hand to shake hers again, this time sincerely. She blushed and her heart raced as she wondered if he knew why she had come. She hesitated, but it was too late.

"I'm all ears. What can I do for you?" he asked gently, leaning in and giving her his full attention.

She paused. She hadn't expected such a receptive audience and needed to compose herself and calculate her next move. She wasn't prepared to share all of the details at once. She wanted to reel him in slowly. Her plan was to offer a few hints about her circumstances and then suggest that a meeting outside of the office would yield a greater reward. She shook her head a couple of times, as though she'd forgotten why she had come in the first place. Hanash cracked a smile. He knew he had her in his grasp. The snake was ready to strike. He stood up and walked over to his closed office door.

"You can tell me whatever you want. No one can hear you behind this door!" he boomed, emphasizing his point that her secrets would be safe inside these walls.

She stared into space and thought carefully, searching for the easiest way to divulge why she had come. Hanash watched as the expression on her face changed. The confidence she had strode in with gave way to a pout and she cast her eyes to the floor. She took a few quick breaths. He knew she was trying to keep her composure. He moved back around his desk and pushed the button on his phone to mute so that they wouldn't be interrupted. He could tell she was searching for a way to seem unrehearsed.

"I don't know where to start."

"Start from the beginning."

She took a beautifully embroidered kerchief from her purse and clutched it nervously. "Better to start from the end. My husband was kidnapped."

He understood intuitively that what was most important was not her husband's kidnapping, but the way in which the kidnapping would be resolved. She gave him the information, piece by piece, monitoring his reactions. This was curious to Hanash because it was the same conversational tactic the big-time drug dealers used. They would give clipped, half-sentence responses to see if their interrogator responded. And they were never in a rush. They knew that the development of the case was dependent upon every little detail they decided to share.

"What is your husband's name?" Detective Hanash asked firmly.

"Mohamed bin Bushuayb, known as al-Sabliyuni."

The detective sat back, taking his time. He was bothered by the fact that he had never heard this name before. "Is he currently living in Tangier?" he asked, as though they had been friends forever.

"He's from Katama, like me, but we were living in Spain."

This cut to the heart of the matter: Katama was a world-renowned hash paradise. He nodded, indicating that her message had been received. "Do you have a picture of him?" he asked.

There was a long silence, as if he had asked her to divulge something off limits. He turned to his computer and typed something, looking at the screen. She searched in her purse, and took out a small picture that had been in a side pocket. She looked at it adoringly before handing it over to him. Detective

Hanash stared at it intently, as though this man were his sworn enemy even before meeting him. Bushra bit her lip, convinced that she had just entangled herself in something grave. Detective Hanash knew exactly what her movements meant: that this was the beginning of an agreement between them.

"Do you know his kidnappers?" he asked nonchalantly, as if he knew the answer in advance.

"No" she said, trying hard to chart an ambiguous route.

He shook his head, knowing what she was up to. "How did you find out he was kidnapped?"

"One of them called me and warned me not to talk to the police. My husband spoke as well, and asked me not to call them. I know I'm not supposed to be here, but here I am."

"What did the kidnappers request from you?"

"A briefcase, but I have no idea where it is."

He got up from his desk and took a seat next to her.

"What's your husband's line of work?" he asked with a sense of gravity that warned her not to lie.

"I don't know exactly. I'm just a housewife. We were living in Marbella and then moved here just five months ago. And then my husband was kidnapped."

She sniffled, choked up, and looked as though she were about to start sobbing.

"If I understand you correctly, you want to get your husband back," he said with feigned empathy. "The kidnappers asked you to hand over a briefcase and you don't know where it is."

She nodded without looking up at him.

Hanash was struck by the gall of this woman. What she had divulged so far lacked cohesion. He hadn't yet pressured her or asked follow-up questions as he would in a real interrogation. He wanted to give her a sense of assurance and listen to her without suspicion, but his years of working with criminals had taught him not to trust what she was saying. He knew she was testing him to see if he would reveal anything he knew about her husband.

She sensed that Hanash was figuring her out and starting to read her thoughts.

"I think your husband is engaged in illegal activities," he said, which clearly took her by surprise.

He was extremely polite in how he crafted this accusation. She went silent for a moment, not knowing how to respond. She knew that whatever she said next would be filed away by Hanash. She muttered some incomprehensible, barely audible remark and then shut up, thinking it better to not even venture a comment. Her mood had changed completely.

Detective Hanash returned to his desk. She did not look like a grieving woman whose husband had been kidnapped by a gang. Her outfit, composed of items from famous Spanish designer boutiques, suggested someone who clearly had other intentions in visiting the office of Tangier's most notorious detective.

3

DETECTIVE HANASH WOULD MEET UP with Bushra whenever she visited Casablanca, putting her up in a secret apartment he owned downtown. Whenever she came down from Tangier he would take time off work. He would tell his family that he had some urgent business and would leave without giving a time frame for his return. This particular time he claimed that he was needed in Fez—taking advantage of the news of a recent spree of burglaries and murders there.

For some time now, the proprietor of the Hotel Scheherazade had stopped paying the kickback to police so they wouldn't come after its top customers—businessmen who would do anything to avoid scandal and preserve their family life. Any facility that serviced this nightlife—bars, clubs, and broth-els—paid off the police to safeguard their interests, and the rates were higher on weekends and paydays. On these days the scene was particularly lucrative. The parties raged into the morning, and everyone benefited; even the cats and dogs got scraps from half-eaten, decadent meals. The weekend cut was methodically planned between the bosses across the board. Hanash took his rotation every two months, sometimes every three. Anyone who entered this business got paid the same share. Detective Hanash could have delegated someone else to take his place, but he didn't trust anyone not to skim a bit off of his share. Even his closest friend wouldn't hand over more than half the collection.

The street in front of Hotel Scheherazade was swarming with police when Hanash arrived. The police presence and number of vehicles in front of the hotel made it seem like the response to a terrorist operation. A security officer was pacing back and forth on the sidewalk, his attention on the hotel entrance. Another officer was indoors inspecting the guest registry. The men and women outside were separated into two lines as uniformed officers led them in pairs to cars that would take them to the station. Most of the clientele heading to the station were those who couldn't afford to pay, so their arrests were intended to divert attention. The real targets of this operation were the men who were still in their rooms with their mistresses, and who would get to haggle with Hanash when he arrived.

The officer inspecting the hotel's guest registry gave Hanash a proper salute and handed over the registry. Hanash skimmed through it. He paused and looked up at the officer. They both knew instinctively that they would begin with room seven.

The detective knocked on the door to room seven, not giving Hamadi and Nezha time to get dressed before ordering the hotel employee to unlock the door. A young, well-built police officer charged into the room. The detective entered, followed by a uniformed security guard who blocked the door with his wide shoulders. Hanash cast a disgusted look at Hamadi, who barely had time to put his glasses on. He didn't even acknowledge Nezha.

"Police! Are you deaf? I said police!" he barked.

Hamadi stood there shaking, his legs barely able to support him.

The hotel hallways were full of commotion, a mix of women's screams and men's pleading as the team of police took over the place. Nezha was unimpressed. This whole scene was an act from a play she had performed in before. She wasn't concerned at all. She put on her clothes quietly and went to the bathroom, where she peed loudly—an act of defiance. When she returned to the room, though, the young police officer lunged at her, slapping her with such force that she crumpled against the wall. Nezha knew that the real motivation behind the slap was to intimidate and frighten Hamadi. She was just a poor, broke prostitute they wouldn't get a single dirham from. What concerned them was the man with a high-powered job, a reputation, and a family to protect, whom they'd caught red-handed cheating. He was the big catch.

Hamadi was so bewildered that he forgot where he was and how he had gotten there. He began to feel unwell. His lips were dry and he was incredibly thirsty. With great difficulty, he made his way to the bathroom and bent over to place his hands under the tepid water coming out of the decaying faucet. He took a good look at himself in the mirror as Hanash started scolding him like a dog.

"Come over here . . . in front of me, old man."

Hamadi shook his head feebly without lifting his eyes. Filtering into the room were all sorts of sounds: women sobbing, desperate pleas, and other adulterers trying to make deals. There was a prostitute shouting hysterically outside on the street. She was yelling that she needed to be released because she had given her baby sleeping medication and left him home alone. Then came the sound of her being slapped, which put an end to her appeals.

Detective Hanash produced a look of total indifference as he gazed at Hamadi, who appeared humble, as if seeking a pardon. Then Hanash looked at Nezha in disgust. She was sobbing in the corner, her hand over the side of her face that had been slapped.

"Stand up and don't move! And shut up, or I'll bury you alive!" said Hanash angrily.

Nezha's voice trembled and she burst into tears. "Hit me as much as you want, sir, but please don't take me to the station."

The officer squeezed her ear violently, knowing she would barely be able to breathe after this. She felt as if he had ripped it off with a pair of sharp pincers and her body was rising toward the ceiling. He let go of her ear and wiped his hand on his sleeve, warning her with a nod that he would do it again if she so much as opened her mouth. Nezha gulped air, tasting her tears and snot, trying not to collapse.

Hanash did a circuit of the room, noticing sticky tissues near the bed. He smiled wryly, knowing that the time had come for him to deliver the reprimand that he had memorized. He looked at Hamadi, who was sitting there guilt-ridden.

"Aren't you embarrassed?" he started in. "A bank director and a respected father who is cheating on his wife with this piece of dirt who is younger than your youngest daughter! How will you face your wife? Your children? Your colleagues at work? Look at yourself! You didn't even use a condom? Aren't you even afraid of giving some disease to your wife?"

Nezha trembled, furious at Hanash's accusations that she was dirty and disease-ridden.

Hamadi broke down and began sobbing. He looked up at Hanash imploringly.

"Please help me, sir, God protect you," he stammered. "I can't go to the station. . . . How can we reach an agreement?"

Detective Hanash ordered the officer to remove Nezha from the room. He dragged her by the arm and shoved her hard toward the door, where the security guard caught her.

"She can wait in the hallway," the officer said to the guard, and locked the door.

Hamadi gained courage and looked at the detective. "I'll give you a thousand dirhams."

The young officer cackled derisively, displaying the braces on his teeth. He shifted about restlessly, revealing the handcuffs and revolver under his belt.

Hanash glared at Hamadi, enraged. He grabbed Hamadi by the collar and shook him violently.

"Is this what we're worth to you? I bet you lost more money than this on that bitch. . . . If I order them to take you to the station there's no going back, no matter what you pay! And if you're arrested when you leave here there isn't a higher power in the land that will prevent you from being sentenced for infidelity, public intoxication, debauchery, and God knows what else. How will you face your wife, your children, your friends, and your bosses? We are doing you a favor. We want you to avoid prison, to avoid a massive scandal. And you're bartering with us?"

Hamadi bowed his head in silence, and for the first time found himself thinking about his wife. She would never forgive him for infidelity. She would let him rot in prison. And his son Radwan, an engineer, how would he take the news? And his daughter, a university professor married to another professor who happened to be a member of the Islamic party? The scandal would reverberate throughout the community.

"If you aren't in a rush," said Hanash, "we have work to do."

Hamadi stared at his executioners, one by one, and could sense that he was a catch for them. He knew his situation was hopeless. He reached into the pocket of his jacket, which had been lying on the ground, took out all the money in his wallet, and handed it over: three thousand dirhams.

Hanash counted the cash quickly, gave Hamadi a look of satisfaction, and placed the money in his inner jacket pocket.

"Don't leave the room now," he said, "and don't let this slut stay with you. It's best to spend the night here and leave in the morning."

Before Hamadi had time to utter a word in protest the detective had rushed out of the room, headed for another.

Hamadi remained frozen in place, all the color drained from his face. He looked sick and exhausted—dark blue rings had appeared under his eyelids. Had they asked, he would have been willing to write a blank check to avoid scandal. Nezha came back into the room, drew close to him, and kissed his head. Despite her uneasiness, she feigned a smile and sat on the edge of the bed.

"I don't think the guy at the front desk was working with the police. I know him well. Maybe there was a misunderstanding between the police and hotel owner."

Hamadi started to feel a tightness in his chest. Nezha's babbling was making him feel nauseated. He was trembling, not from fear, but because he felt he was getting sick.

"You didn't have to give them all your money. They would have been okay with the thousand dirhams that you first suggested. Trust me, I've seen this before."

Clearly Nezha had overheard what had happened. Hamadi remained in place, silent. He couldn't deal with her right now. He rubbed his bloodshot eyes under his thick-rimmed glasses and felt the fever creep through his body. He stood there, still stunned, unable to even look at Nezha.

"I'm leaving," he said, feeling suffocated. He paused for a moment, holding his keys and waiting for her response.

"Don't you want to stay till the morning as usual?" she asked.

He looked down and shook his head. He stood at the door while Nezha took out a pack of cigarettes and lit up the last one in the pack.

"Can you wait until I finish my cig?" she said angrily as she blew smoke in his direction.

She drew one leg over the other in an attempt to lure him back in, but he turned his back. It was clear to her now that things would never be the same between them. Her generous monthly client was about to vanish into thin air. She then remembered that she didn't even have enough money for a cab home, and there was no way she could ask Hamadi since he had just emptied his entire wallet.

"Can you give me a ride home?"

He didn't even answer her as he left the room.

An amusing scene awaited Detective Hanash in the next room. There was a pretty, polished woman in risqué underwear, accompanied by a young man who could have been her son's age. He was wearing only his underpants, and despite the tense atmosphere in the room, his penis remained hard as a rock. This amused the police so much that they called their boss to come take a look. Hanash was shocked when he saw the guy, and after taking a second to catch his breath, he looked at the woman. She seemed respectable and refined—likely not a prostitute at all. What a catch, especially if she was married! And then there was this young guy, in his underwear, with his weapon standing up. The officers were too distracted by the guy's penis to ask the woman any questions. The woman seemed unshaken. To Hanash, her calmness suggested that she had already been given the okay by another officer.

Hanash looked squarely at the young man and said, "Put down your weapon, you bastard!"

All the officers burst out in laughter. Even the woman couldn't resist a wry smile.

"What can I do? I can't control it," said the young man, shaking from fear.

Everyone started laughing again, and the detective looked at the woman, feigning scorn.

"Didn't you do anything to cool him off? You should have chosen someone closer to your age, madam."

This made the woman blush, but the young man took it as an insult.

"We did it twice," he said.

One of the officers told him to shut up and the young man recoiled, still straight as a spear.

"Did you take Viagra?" Detective Hanash asked.

The young man bristled and fired back at him: "I'm from Dakala, and men from my region are well known for their virility."

Hanash didn't know how to respond to this at first. The young man had crossed the line. How dare he suggest that his manhood was greater than that of Hanash and his men!

"What makes you people so horny is that you've been having sex with animals since you were kids," Hanash quipped.

Everyone laughed, and Hanash ordered the officers to take the man to the station.

"We'll see if he stays like that at the station," said an officer. He pushed him away and a security guard grabbed him.

The detective turned his attention to the woman.

She began explaining, as if she had prepared her statement in advance: "I'm an agricultural engineer who travels a lot for work. One time I visited the agricultural area in Dakala and met this young man, who was working in the fields. I've been divorced for three years . . . and when it comes to my body, just like anyone else, it's my right to do what I want. Since getting divorced I hadn't been with anyone until I met this guy a month ago. I was really scared, and I know what I did was wrong, but it just happened. I got in touch with him, and he brought me to this place. I'm responsible for what happened and I'll pay whatever you suggest."

Hanash was confused by her story. It got him thinking about his wife, whom he hadn't even touched in months. Sometimes he'd see her putting on makeup and jewelry. Was she getting ready to meet up with a secret lover somewhere? He was silent for a minute as he contemplated the woman in front of him in her underwear. He told her to wrap something around herself. She got dressed quickly, putting on a long dress. She was a bit chunky, and the scars from a cesarean section were still visible on her soft belly. She wasn't beautiful but certainly wasn't unattractive either.

Hanash felt a sense of empathy overcome him, and his anger began to subside. He believed her story.

"Why did you come with him to *this* place? Couldn't you have found somewhere else?" he asked.

"He picked the place. It would have been tough for me to turn back after we were already in the room. And this isn't my city. I had intended to get out of here early, before you all showed up. But, well, look how things turned out."

Hanash took out his cell phone and ordered the officers not to take the young man to the station. If they did, they would have to take her as well. She nodded at him in appreciation.

He watched her carefully as she took out her purse, ready to pay.

"What's the amount?" she asked, as if she were at the cash register in a grocery store.

"Who told you I take bribes?" he asked. "I could add a bribery charge in addition to debauchery."

She nodded and looked at him. "You can do whatever you want with me, sir. Send me to prison, or ruin my reputation in front of my son, daughter, family, colleagues. But I'm telling you I wouldn't be able to carry on like that—scandalized. I'd rather die. I'd kill myself."

"Didn't you think about that before you took off your clothes?"

She sighed and wiped her hands on her dress. "I can't even explain to *myself* how this happened," she said. "I battled with these feelings and then they took control. Our souls are dark caves, unknown even to us."

"Many criminals would say the same thing," he said. "In our line of work, we don't care about someone's motivations. We don't accept someone justifying their actions with emotions that they claim clouded their judgment. The law only acknowledges what someone has done, but the reasons and motivations are outside the frame. Right now, you're in it deep. Knowing *how* you fell so deep won't help you at all."

She felt her body temperature rising suddenly, and she went back to the drawing board, trying to think of another way out of this predicament.

"I have a lot of money in the bank," she said confidently, as she took her bank card out. "I'll let you have my password," she said, offering him the card. "I'll write it down. You can take whatever you want and keep me here until you get back."

Hanash crossed his arms and gave her a little smile. "I don't accept ATM cards."

He had never met a woman like this in a cheap prostitute's haunt. The usual way things went down in these situations was that there was a lot of cursing, insulting, slapping, and kicking. He thought that if he had met this woman in another context he would have spoken to her with respect and admiration. He also thought that if he hadn't caught her with this village boy in this dirty place, but under different circumstances, he might want her for himself. She was different: she was cultured, an engineer, and had a strong personality. She was the antithesis of all the women he had met in these contexts before.

"How much money do you have with you?" he asked, his voice starting to soften from fatigue.

She emptied the contents of her purse on the bed. It was a mixture of makeup, crumpled receipts, and other trivial things. She grabbed a bunch of bills and handed them over . . . it wasn't as much as he anticipated.

"That's all an engineer carries with her?"

She paused for a moment, recalling something that would save her some extra time and effort. She opened an interior pocket of her handbag and pulled out a gold necklace that had a shiny precious stone.

"This is extremely valuable and worth more than anything I could give you. It's all yours."

He took the necklace. "I'll consider it a gift," he said, running his fingers over the stone.

4

THE CALL TO PRAYER RANG out at daybreak in Kandahar, the name the residents of Casablanca's Saada district gave their neighborhood. The muezzin, Driss, had a beautiful and gentle voice. The mosque didn't have a speaker or a minaret, so designating it a mosque was something of an exaggeration. The "mosque" was really a garage on the ground floor of a building owned by a Moroccan émigré who lived abroad. He had Belgian citizenship and had joined an extremist group to fight the Russians in Afghanistan; then he fought the Americans with the Taliban. After Kabul fell, all the fighters received orders to return home and await instructions regarding future operations. Most Moroccans came back, but those holding European citizenship were told to gather donations and start funding mosques in impoverished and marginalized neighborhoods, like this one in Kandahar. As far as the extremists were concerned, state-registered mosques were off limits for prayer since they were not seen to be built on real piety—not to mention all the informants, lackeys, and spies that infiltrated them.

The owner of this building followed his orders. Each year, he would return from Europe more of a fanatic. He entrusted the mosque to a group of young men primed for radicalizing others and who had nothing more to pin their hopes on than waging jihad.

The Kandahar neighborhood was located in the heart of Casablanca, the nation's economic capital and home to over four million residents. It was uniquely positioned, set between soaring high-rises on one side and massive elegant villas on the other. It was an ugly stain on the urban fabric, with its dirty walls, draped doorways, and unbearable stench. The haphazard construction, the tin-panel roofs everywhere, and trash strewn all over made it seem like a neighborhood that had been hit by a tornado. A home built to house a single family was partitioned into four, and more closely resembled a rabbit's den: no windows, no kitchen, and no facilities whatsoever. Families piled together in the quarters at night to sleep, but during the day most activity took place by the entryways, where the clotheslines were strung. True suffering came to the neighborhood in the winter months, when rain turned the unpaved passageways into mud, and the winds carried plastic bags and other light rubbish their way. In the summer, residents had to battle insects, cockroaches, rats, stray dogs, and putrid smells.

The neighborhood was completely deserted and still pitch black at this early hour. Everyone was asleep except those at the mosque, which was located at one end of the neighborhood.

It was lit with neon lights and plastic mats covered the floor. It didn't have any openings except for its wide wooden door, which allowed for some air circulation. All of those praying were neighborhood youth—many wearing Afghani attire, consisting of a short tunic over trousers, and sneakers. Most of them had beards, but had refrained from growing moustaches. After the early-morning prayer everyone dispersed and headed home to go back to bed, except three young friends: Driss the muezzin; Sufyan, who was preparing to travel to Syria to become a martyr; and Ibrahim, Nezha's brother. They had gotten used to hanging around after prayer under the streetlight at the edge of the neighborhood, where they discussed religion, politics, and jihad. They were all close in age. Sufyan was the eldest, at only twenty-four years old. He planned to travel to Syria via Turkey in a couple of days to carry out his mission.

Sufyan was considered the religious leader of the neighborhood. He was skinny and rigidly built, and sported a thick beard. He was anxious and fidgety. He had been expelled from school, and before turning to religion he had been addicted to all sorts of substances: hash, hallucinogens, and any cheap alcohol. When he got drunk or high he'd take off his shirt to show off his muscles, and parade through the neighborhood brandishing a sword, waving it in everyone's face. It was impossible for anyone to stop him, and no one in the neighborhood dared call the police, fearing revenge.

Everything changed when Sufyan's mother passed away. She died in his arms, after suffering from cancer for years without ever even knowing about it. She had never received proper health care, and couldn't afford to go to the hospital. A nurse in the neighborhood clinic had diagnosed her condition from her symptoms. Sufyan would give her aspirin to ease her pain during the toughest times, when the pain was tearing up her insides. She underwent herbal treatments, and would visit revered herbalists and so-called miracle workers, who claimed to be capable of treating anything. Her health worsened day after day until she began falling in and out of consciousness. Sufyan was by her side until the moment she passed.

Sufyan was so deeply affected by his mother's death that he left the neighborhood for an entire year. When he returned, he was a completely different young man. He wore Afghani attire, sported a thick, rough beard, and espoused extremist views. He declared that his new mission was the promotion of Islamic virtue and prevention of vice. He had a real impact on the youth of the neighborhood, who came to listen to him, and then began to admire and respect him. He showed how religion could transform the immorality and violence of your past into a life of piety and salvation. No one knew—not even his two best friends, Ibrahim and Driss—where he had spent that year away. When asked, he would look into the distance and offer a calm smile. His gaze would wander as if he were in another world, and he'd just say he was with "the group," giving no further details.

On the opposite end of the spectrum from Sufyan's desire for leadership and power was Ibrahim, Nezha's brother. He wasn't self-assured: even in the company of his friends he was introverted. He listened far more than he spoke, despite the fact that he had spent half a year at university. His mind wandered whenever Sufyan assailed them with some new religious treatise. He would pretend to be listening and feign interest, meanwhile absorbed in his own conflicted and depressive state. Deep down he was not religious, and didn't even have much desire to pray, but he feared he would be cut off from the neighborhood gang if he deviated from their views. This close-knit group was hostile to anyone who left—considering him or her an apostate. Ibrahim needed to maintain their acceptance and friendship, so he wouldn't be kicked out, but he also needed it to distance himself from his sister Nezha's conduct. He was ready to respond forcefully to any insinuation that she wasn't proper and chaste. He insisted that his sister—even if she wore makeup and wasn't veiled—was just an employee at a clothing factory.

Driss, whom Sufyan had chosen to be the muezzin because of his melodious voice, was the youngest of the three, only twenty-one years old. He looked like a burly kid: he had exaggerated features and colorless, aggressive eyes. He claimed to know absolutely everything in spite of his obvious ignorance, and he never hesitated to argue passionately with anyone who disagreed with Sufyan. Driss was expelled from school by sixth grade after failing repeatedly. In his teenage years he followed the same path as Sufyan: he took any cheap drug he could get his hands on, he picked pockets in the market, and his family kicked him out so many times that he was basically homeless.

Sufyan took him under his wing after returning from his year with "the group," and since then, Driss and Sufyan were attached at the hip, like a student clinging to his sheikh.

The three stood there under the lamppost, which went out with the first crack of sunlight, discussing Sufyan's preparations for his trip to Syria in a couple of days. This had to be kept a complete secret. Before Ibrahim was able to ask Sufyan about the latest arrangements, Sufyan dove into an explanation of Driss's recent dream, in which he had seen a candle.

"A candle appearing in a dream is a good sign, especially if it is brightly lit," Sufyan explained, enthusiastically assuming the role of a mufti, and gesticulating wildly. "For a bachelor it means a wife is on the horizon. For a married man, it means children. For someone lost, it means divine guidance. And for the poor, it means wealth. But if the flame is dim, that is evidence of weakness, but it will still lead you to the right path."

"Sufyan, what book did you read this interpretation in?" Ibrahim asked in a sleepy voice, hoping to show interest even though he already knew the answer.

"*The Interpretation of Dreams* by Ibn Sirin."

Sufyan's reply to Ibrahim was authoritative and gruff, and he immediately turned his attention back to Driss, probing him as if pushing him to confess to something he wasn't comfortable with. This was the third time in less than a week that Driss had asked for the explanation of the candle dream. Sufyan wondered if he was trying to tell him something. Was there some secret causing this repeated inquiry? Sufyan crossed his arms, a position he adopted only when he was about to give a prognostication.

"Be honest with me, Driss," he said, tightening his lips and coughing. "You know there is no shame in faith. Are you playing with yourself?"

Ibrahim couldn't hold back a smirk, but a stern look from Sufyan paralyzed him. Driss turned around, pretending to spit in the corner. He had to answer, but he was always pitiful when talking about anything personal.

"What do you mean, Sufyan?"

"I mean, are you masturbating?"

Driss was clearly frustrated, but he tried to seem calm. It was just as hard for him to tell a lie as it was to confess. Driss remained silent, and then Sufyan started in on his legal opinion, like he was reading straight from a book.

"Masturbation, brothers, is prohibited in the sharia for men and women, the married and unmarried, due to its unhealthy repercussions. If semen is produced, proper cleansing must follow. The best way to rid yourself of this habit is abstinence, and then by seeking marriage, through God's guidance. We need to understand that it is prohibited and resist these urges, just as we need to constantly remember our own mortality.

"Resist the urge, and stop this altogether," Sufyan said, laying a hand on Driss's shoulder.

Ibrahim tried to hide his smirk again. He was concerned that Sufyan was going to begin questioning him, so he beat him to it, by speaking up quickly to change the subject. Ibrahim asked about the war in Iraq and Syria, a topic Sufyan never tired of, and asked how his travel preparations were coming along.

"I received orders to be extra cautious," Sufyan said, answering him curtly. "There are spies all over the neighborhoods that send fighters to Syria and Iraq."

Driss spat in the corner. "Death to traitors, spies, and state security!" he proclaimed heatedly.

"I will depart soon, inshallah, with the help of our brothers," Sufyan said quietly. "When I arrive I'll get my mission, along with the brothers arriving from all over the Islamic world."

"I'd love to die as a martyr in Iraq or Syria," Driss said, looking at Sufyan with admiration.

"Your turns will come soon, inshallah," Sufyan said, patting Driss on the shoulder and gesturing toward Ibrahim.

"True Islam won't be achieved," Sufyan said passionately, "until the Islamic State, with its capital of Baghdad, is established. Islam is an all-encompassing system that governs every single aspect of life, and is intended for everyone. Islam guides the individual, the sword conquers and subjugates, and the tank and warplane kill those who renounce Islam while coercing others to embrace it. Islam is a faith that supersedes other faiths present in this world, and therefore there is no use in considering interfaith dialogue or peacefully coexisting. The mujahideen are striving to eliminate all political systems because each is an embodiment of the false idols the Quran commands us to destroy. Jihad is the only way we can establish God's kingdom on earth, and martyring yourself by blowing yourself up allows you to reach the highest rungs of heaven. Because of that, I'm looking forward to death and meeting my divine maker. I'm going to cross the borders and join the mujahideen. I won't be taken prisoner. I'll enter Syria by God's will and I'll transform my body into a bomb that blasts the enemy into pieces! I'll make their heretical brains—"

He suddenly stopped talking. They'd heard noises, which turned out to be a car parking not too far away. Was it the secret police? After the most recent terrorist attacks that had rocked Casablanca, this neighborhood had been under close observation by the authorities. The three friends froze. The hair on the backs of their necks stood on end as they watched a young woman get out of a Mercedes and slam the door. They made out a gray-haired older man shaking his fist and yelling unintelligibly before racing off.

Nezha raised her head, frozen in place. Her heart was pounding. Standing there with her breasts spilling out of her shirt, wearing a short skirt, and eyes swollen and red, she seemed out of place. She stared at what looked like ghosts under the lamppost. She had not anticipated seeing anyone. She had never returned at this time before, nor in such a scandalous way. Normally when she was out at night she wouldn't return until the next afternoon, with groceries or other necessities in hand, getting dropped off by a cab right in front of their house—and then disappearing inside in an instant. But right now, she was completely exposed in the early-morning light, and there was no turning back. She had no idea what would come of this. She lowered her head, pulled her dress down—it barely covered half of her thighs anyway—and tried her best not to stagger. She had no choice but to pass within a few steps of them. She smiled in an attempt to drive back the fear that coursed through her, and walked past them. Had she been able to look up, she would have seen her brother Ibrahim. His eyes were bulging out of their sockets and burning with rage. His face was ashen and he was short of breath as sweat began to bead on his forehead. The feelings of shame were more than he could bear. His muscles tensed and all the emotion paralyzed him. Nezha continued walking in her high heels. Sufyan and Driss didn't stop watching until she disappeared into the house.

Ibrahim remained as still as a statue.

Sufyan cleared his throat and tugged on his thick beard, as if he wanted to pull it out.

"Before we think about jihad in Iraq and Syria," Sufyan said in a calm voice, "we need to wage jihad in our own neighborhood. This just confirms that we have been right all along. And now you've seen, Ibrahim, with your own eyes, the state of your sister. And the nerve of that driver! Dropping her off like that in our neighborhood."

"If that was my sister, I'd kill her," said Driss, shaking with rage as he looked at Ibrahim.

Ibrahim said nothing. Despair and depression were written all over his pale face. How he wished for a cigarette right now, despite having quit years ago. His friends' words felt like nails being hammered into his head, and he couldn't change the subject this time. He opened his mouth to say something but Sufyan cut him off sternly, as if he had no right to speak.

"How many times did I warn you, Ibrahim, to keep an eye on your sister, to tell her to stop wearing makeup and force her to wear the veil?"

Ibrahim looked up, still unable to believe what had happened.

"Kandahar is one of the most virtuous neighborhoods in the city, and one of its women returns drunk and half naked at daybreak? By God, the All-Powerful, who will rid this neighborhood of its filth?" Sufyan kept repeating himself and pacing, beating his chest feverishly. Then he glared disapprovingly at Ibrahim. "Do you know what a diyouth is, Ibrahim?"

"A diyouth is someone who sees evil in his own family and doesn't do anything about it," Driss jumped in, directing his scorn at Ibrahim.

Ibrahim raged inside. He wanted to respond to Driss, but couldn't find his voice—it betrayed him. He was overcome by such intense rage that he started imagining himself beating his sister, kicking her, even stabbing her. He couldn't handle any more blame from his friends, and thought that if he stuck around he might get in a fight with them. He said his goodbyes, lowered his head, and headed home. He walked with determination, ready to do something serious.

Ibrahim opened the door and gave a quick look toward his sister's room, which appeared to be quiet and pitch black. He felt that something had happened before he arrived. His mother was sleeping, or pretending to be asleep, in her usual corner of the basement-level apartment. The only real room in the house was Nezha's room, since the rest of the place more closely resembled a cellar: a few square feet without any windows or openings whatsoever. His mother, Ruqiya, repositioned herself, groaning painfully, as she battled intense pain. She was a worn-out soul and was extremely skinny. She looked like someone who had borne the brunt of an incredibly difficult life. Her husband's passing four years ago coincided with the onset of kidney problems that flared up with the slightest aggravation. Everyone walked on eggshells around her, and luckily she had Nezha and Ibrahim to take care of her. Ibrahim would kiss her forehead and hand after waking, and before sleeping. He would jump to get her what she needed, sometimes before she even asked.

Ibrahim tried to compose himself as he listened to his mother's moaning. He had no doubt that Nezha had told their mother what happened before she holed up in her room. Certainly his mother was aware of the humiliation Ibrahim suffered in front of his friends. Were his mother's moans this time the result of kidney pain shooting through her side, or was she faking, fearful of Ibrahim's reaction? She knew that the one thing Ibrahim wouldn't do was agitate her and cause her even more pain. Her latest episode had passed only a few days ago, and she was still recovering.

Ibrahim slumped down in the corner and closed his eyes, denying himself an impulsive response. He was conflicted as to what to do. A dark cloud of depression overcame him as he recalled what his friends had said: "A diyouth is someone who sees evil in his own family and doesn't do anything."

He had believed, or at least let himself believe, that his sister worked nights at a clothing factory. It was no secret that she was the sole provider for the family, so he was in no position to ask questions. He pretended to sleep, even placing a pillow over his head, as if that would help him avoid reality. He remembered how he had been able to attend university for six months thanks to his "seamstress" sister. And then, when things got bad financially and he had to withdraw, he wanted to take up his father's stall in the neighborhood market. The competitors kicked him out, insisting that his father had never had a permanent spot. He had been unemployed since then, a total waste of space. It was only in connecting with his religious friends that he restored some purpose to life, not to mention simply having something to do. He spent his day between the mosque and hanging about with other unemployed people in the neighborhood, and he always had a hot meal when he returned home. But now, how was he going to deal with this? How would he face his friends at the mosque tomorrow? Could he spend time with them after they called him a diyouth? If he didn't take revenge on his sister to restore his honor then he wouldn't be a man. A strong desire seized him to head straight to the kitchen, get out a knife, and cut her throat as she slept. But then he thought about his mother kneeling in front of him, trying to block his path, and reaching out, begging him to stop. This isn't the time, he said to himself, and tried to go to sleep.

Nezha normally spent the morning hours asleep, and she didn't wake until three or four in the afternoon. She would have a meal with her mother and then prep for another night out. She would shower, get dressed, tie her hair back, and leave the house looking like she was going to a normal job. She'd then head straight to Salwa's Salon, which she considered a second home. It was there that she would get her hair done and put on makeup, in preparation for the evening. Most nights she would end her evening right after midnight, except for Fridays and Saturdays. When she returned home on weeknights she'd find the neighborhood empty. The taxi would drop her off right at her door, and with a couple of steps she'd be inside. No one would be up to greet her at that time. Her mother was either asleep, or trying to sleep. If Ibrahim was awake when he heard the taxi door shut, he'd hide his head under the covers. When she stayed out all night she usually didn't return until the next day, around midday, when she could unassumingly disappear into the commotion of the neighborhood.

She awoke to the sound of her phone ringing out a familiar tune. She looked at the clock. It was four thirty in the afternoon. She felt exhausted and didn't want to get out of bed. She closed her eyes and thought about what had happened yesterday. Everything flashed in front of her like a scene from a horror movie. She cursed the police, who ruined everything. She hadn't been paid because of them, and that had thwarted her plans to solve her financial issues with Farqash. What she feared even more, though, was him sending the glue-sniffing street kids after her. She put her hands to her face and coiled into a fetal position, starting to tear up at the thought. The anguish involved in just thinking about what Farqash would do to her made her forget about the nasty slap she'd received the day before from the policeman, not to mention her ear, and the feeling that it had nearly been ripped off. All of this pain for nothing! She didn't even have cash to buy a pack of cigarettes, or to leave money for her mother before heading out again.

She felt, for the first time, that the burden she carried was too heavy to bear alone. Why had her father died when he did? If he were still alive she might be in university now. She was filled with sadness as she remembered her time in school. She had been a devoted and outstanding student in her humanities classes. She always scored the highest grade on compositions. Her Arabic teacher even told her she had a promising future in writing. He encouraged her to try to write her own stories. She enjoyed writing short stories and creating her own characters, but mostly she enjoyed the attention from her teacher.

Her Arabic teacher was close to fifty and lived alone. One day, he invited her to stop by his home to give her some novels. At the time, she hadn't even considered the fact that he didn't have a wife or children, but after he opened the door, it was clear that he was not quite so clean-cut as she had thought. There were wine bottles everywhere, the ashtrays were jam-packed with cigarette butts, and newspapers and books were strewn all around, in every nook and cranny. She thought he might throw himself on her at the first opportunity, but he sat there facing her, opened a novel, and began to read to her: "She met him under the trees that evening. Rain began falling when he kissed her for the first time. He drew her in, and their bodies joined . . ." She didn't even remember how he shifted from reading to kissing her.

She remembered fondly this first love affair with her teacher. She was just shy of sixteen at the time. She was poor, but had dreams: her major aspiration was to obtain a bachelor's degree and then travel far away from where she lived—from this neighborhood riddled with violence and conflict. All the young men smoked cheap hash, took the hallucinogen called qarqubi, and drank spoiled wine, after which they drew their swords and knives and fought like dogs. Sufyan, the most dangerous one, was infatuated with her. Each night, after the qarqubi took effect, he'd lose control, strip off his shirt, and wave his sword around, spreading fear through the neighborhood. No one dared challenge or resist him, fearing his retribution. Nezha was the only one who knew the real secret behind all of his antics. She knew that he was head over heels for her. He used to send her love letters that were filled with grammatical errors and didn't make any sense. But Sufyan never assailed her or even made a move on her. He was well aware that the repercussions of a romantic relationship between a boy and girl from Kandahar could ruin the girl's family.

While it seemed like ages ago to Nezha, it had only been a few years since a wave of religious radicalization had taken over the youth. The young men turned away from drugs and toward strict religious observance and extreme views. They exchanged one form of violence for another—observing prayer was vigorously enforced, girls were coerced to don the veil, and men were forced to wear Afghani clothing and grow beards. Outsiders rarely entered the neighborhood. If they got lost and somehow ended up there, they would be interrogated and, in some cases, attacked. The youth liked to think of Kandahar as one of the "free zones" of the city—free from outsiders and the intrusion of the government. Nezha thought about all of this as she contemplated the agony she had put her brother through that morning. She already knew that most of their neighbors had their doubts about her supposed job, and were just waiting for her to slip up. She figured that her mother and brother also had their doubts.

She lay there and listened closely, unable to leave the bed. A strange silence filled the house. Usually when she slept this late into the afternoon her mother would knock on the door and ask, in a soft voice, "Aren't you going to get up?" and Nezha would reply, "I'm awake, Mom."

Where had her mother gone? Why such utter silence? Nezha reached out and turned on the lamp. There wasn't a window in the room, and only a hole above the doorway leading to the living room allowed for a bit of air circulation. Despite this, her room was the nicest in the house—if one could call it a house. Her room had a real bed, a small dresser with a mirror on top, and a makeup counter. Nezha sat on the edge of the bed, put her head between her hands, and thought about what she had done. What had happened yesterday would have consequences. Fear gripped her as she thought about what might happen now. She clutched her cell phone, and after a brief hesitation punched in Salwa's number.

"Hello . . . Salwa, are you at the salon?" she whispered.

"Yeah. Are you still at home?"

"Yup, I'm at home. Do you have anyone right now?"

"I have a customer, but I'll be done in about fifteen minutes. I can barely hear you. How was last night? Everything okay?"

Nezha was desperate to tell her friend what had happened at the hotel last night and then what had happened that morning, but she held back.

"I'm all right. We'll talk when I get there," she said quickly.

She hung up without waiting for a reply. She opened the door to the living room, which was also pitch black. Why hadn't her mother opened the door and opened the drapes yet? Nezha felt depressed, as if she were seeing for the very first time the prison cell she called home. She went to the bathroom and then got dressed quickly. She desperately wanted a cigarette. At this point, she didn't even care where her mother was or about her brother's reaction. But as she was putting on her shoes, the door opened and her mother and brother came in. Nezha stood up and put her hands out in front of her face, fearing that her brother was going to slap her. He had hit her a couple of times because he didn't think her clothes were conservative enough, or because she refused to wear a veil.

"Where were you yesterday?" he snarled at her, pulsing with anger.

Her mother groaned and collapsed on the bed. Nezha looked at her, but her mother averted her eyes and continued groaning, leaving Nezha feeling deserted.

"What type of job do you come home from looking like a whore?"

These words rang out painfully, and a look of utter astonishment spread over Nezha's face. Had they *really* believed that she was working at a factory? Had they only just discovered her real job? She was so surprised that she didn't know how to reply.

"Who was the guy who dropped you off?" asked Ibrahim, getting angrier by the moment.

"He's the owner of the factory I work at. There weren't any other options at that time."

Their mother sat up and looked at Ibrahim.

"This is what I told you, son. We need to hear her out first."

"Do you believe her?"

Their mother went back to groaning. Pain shot through her as though someone were hammering on her spine, and she placed her hands on her lower back. Ibrahim looked over at her as his frustration welled up. On the one hand, his anger at his sister was burning him up inside; on the other hand, he didn't want to cause his mother further pain and have to take her back to the hospital.

Their mother slumped down again and Nezha tended to her, helping her stretch her legs out.

"Are you all right, Mom?"

"What am I supposed to do? Yesterday I thought I was going to die. . . . If only I had. I didn't sleep a wink last night. I kept hearing your brother toss and turn. God save us from the youth in this neighborhood. Their sole occupation is to make up lies about people."

She looked at her son to see what effect her words had on him. His expression frightened her—he was pale, his lips were cracked, and his face was taut. He gave her a blank stare, indicating his absolute refusal to participate in this charade. For the first time, his mother felt like she didn't know her son. He seemed to her to be completely distraught and unaware of what he was saying. Nezha sensed the same thing. Then, suddenly, he fell silent, as if he had come up with a new way to deal with this situation. And from the grim look on his face, it didn't seem like a good thing. Without saying a word, he shook his head threateningly, retreated toward the door, and left the house.

Nezha and her mother exchanged perplexed looks.

"Mom, I didn't get paid yesterday," she said, to change the subject.

"Why, Nezha? We're drowning in debts—the pharmacy, groceries, rent. We have nothing to eat tonight. Your brother and I had to walk home from the hospital because we couldn't even pay for a bus ticket."

"I'm doing my best!" Nezha exploded. "Why doesn't *he* work? He's the man! He spends all day with that group of jobless losers at the top of the street telling us what's halal and what's haram. Is that what being religious means? If he was actually concerned about my honor and dignity then he'd roll up his sleeves and look for a job."

Her mother fell silent and didn't offer a reply. Nezha continued to get herself ready to leave.

"Maybe I'll get paid tonight," she said wearily. She bent over to kiss her mother on the forehead as she always did before leaving. Her mother was infuriated, and closed her eyes, not even saying her usual "May God guide you."

Nezha headed out feeling like she had the weight of the world on her shoulders. She walked hurriedly, with her head down. She felt like the whole neighborhood was watching her from windows, doorways, and around corners. She mustered the courage to look up, and in the distance saw her brother standing by the lamppost with Driss, who she really hated. She knew that Sufyan was also watching her from the roof of his family's house. She feared that someone would attack her. She wouldn't feel safe until she made it out of the neighborhood and could be swallowed up by the busy thoroughfare. She picked up her pace and was now nearly running toward Salwa's Salon.

The salon was tiny, like a small convenience store, and had a cozy atmosphere. It was located about two blocks from Kandahar, in an area that the religious zealots didn't control. It occupied the first floor of a two-story building and had a tinted glass façade. The sign said "closed," even though it was open. On the walls were large posters of women with different hairstyles. Inside, there was just one chair in front of a mirror, a tattered sofa, and a table with old magazines on it.

Salwa was thirty-five and sported brash, bleached-blonde hair that she tied back. Her makeup wasn't able to cover up her extremely pale complexion. She was divorced and supported her two children and her half-blind grandmother. A few years ago her salon was the most popular one in the area. But then salons started getting a bad reputation. Men began prohibiting their wives from going to them, and rumors spread about hairstylists colluding with pimps to encourage pretty young women to go into prostitution.

Salwa was waiting impatiently for Nezha. She kissed her on both cheeks as she walked in the door and then grabbed her hand and pulled her inside, locking the glass door behind them. Nezha sat on the couch and Salwa plunked herself down in the styling chair.

"Can you order me a coffee and give me a cigarette?"

Salwa placed a pack of cigarettes in front of her and called to order a coffee from the café next door. She waited until Nezha had lit the cigarette and taken a few quick drags.

"What happened?" Salwa asked. "I didn't like the tone of your voice when you called."

Nezha, trying hard to hold back tears, started describing her night. She detailed the previous day's events, especially her horrifying encounter with the police, and embellished a bit as she went. Salwa didn't interrupt her except to open the door for the waiter who brought Nezha's coffee. When Nezha arrived at the incident that happened at daybreak, Salwa rushed to the door to take a look outside.

"I'm scared of an attack," Salwa said. "I've thought a lot about leaving this area. If it weren't for my kids, I wouldn't stay another night." She slouched into the styling chair. "I get letters every day demanding that I close the salon and start wearing a veil," she went on. "I've gotten plenty of phone calls from people urging me to close the 'Prostitute Club,' as they call it. They urge me to repent and return to God, as if I'm a nonbeliever."

Nezha lit another cigarette, inhaled deeply, and drank the last sip of coffee. She rose, went to the mirror, and inspected herself closely.

"Why do I have such bad luck?" she asked, addressing herself in the mirror.

Salwa smiled to herself and sighed. At the end of the day, Nezha was still just an innocent young woman whose life circumstances had placed her in difficult situations.

"My income this month is zero," said Nezha. "I was depending on Hamadi, and now everything is busted. Screw the police!"

"I heard that the raid yesterday was extensive, and that the station is full of girls."

Nezha sat in the styling chair that Salwa had just gotten up from, and checked her hair.

"I wish the police had arrested me so I wouldn't have run into my brother and his friends when I got back," she said.

Salwa began to comb Nezha's hair.

"Don't pay attention to your brother," said Salwa. "Doesn't he know that you go out? If he was a real man he'd be looking for a job. I don't get those guys who spend their days at the mosque or bumming around all day in the streets. They don't seem to care about their parents slaving away. Is that religion? The Prophet, peace be upon him, commanded us to work. Honorable work, of course."

"And if we can't find honorable work?"

"You want my opinion?" said Salwa. "Even your job is honorable. You go out with men to help your sick mother. If there is anyone at fault here it's your brother—he's lazy and dependent."

"He did go to university and tried to take our father's place in the market, but they prevented him."

"He should have fought harder to find *any* job, for your sake and your mother's sake. He hasn't got an excuse."

Salwa continued combing Nezha's hair, feeling really worked up. Nezha was a bit taken aback by how intensely Salwa criticized Ibrahim.

"My brother is really shy and will avoid conflict at all costs," Nezha said. "I feel like he's tortured but doesn't know what to do. He went everywhere looking for a job after our father passed. He even sold individual cigarettes and shined shoes as a university student. But he's shy. God knows what Sufyan and Driss said to him when they saw Hamadi dropping me off, half naked and drunk, right in front of them."

"Be careful, sister. Your brother hangs out with the 'Afghans,' as they call them."

"If not for my mother, I wouldn't have gone home."

Salwa turned on the hair dryer to finish shaping Nezha's hair, its loud hum drowning out their conversation.

Nezha sat quietly while Salwa teased and styled. She thought about the first time she'd met Salwa, and how that meeting had changed her life. Salwa's father had died unexpectedly following a botched operation. Afterward, the family's financial situation got worse by the day. Salwa stopped going to school and took to the streets in search of a job. Whenever she found one, she learned that she had to do something 'extra' to get it. One time, one of her bosses assaulted her right in his office, ripping off her underwear and nearly raping her. He only stopped when she screamed. He slapped her, called her a young whore, told her she was out of line, and threw her out of his office. She wasn't able to get a job without using her body. She considered submitting to this reality, but felt they would get rid of her as soon as they had their way. What they all wanted was her young body—a child's body, really—since she wasn't even sixteen at that time.

As a result, Salwa didn't keep up the job search for very long. She began spending all her time wandering from one store to the next trying to sell toothpaste on behalf of some company, barely making enough to get by. One day while she was out selling, a boy mugged her, hitting her in the face and stealing her bag, leaving her with nothing.

Eventually Salwa was able to get her affairs in order and open a small salon. The salon gained a bad reputation in the neighborhood, and everyone, including Nezha, heard how husbands forbade their wives from visiting it. But Nezha was curious about Salwa and her salon, and one morning she decided to head there. Salwa welcomed Nezha into the salon and got right to down to business.

"You have a gorgeous body. Why not take advantage of it before giving it up to some loser for nothing?"

Nezha was startled by Salwa's directness, and as she started to reply Salwa approached, grabbed her by the hand, and sat her in the very same styling chair that she was sitting in now.

"I've known you since you were a baby," she said. "Ruqiya, your mom, cleaned houses and your father, Mohamed, may he rest in peace, had a stall in the market. Your brother wasn't able to take his place—may God help you all. Times are tough, but if you want me to help, I can help."

Salwa inspected Nezha from head to toe. "If you're busy and you need to go, come back another time."

"No. I'm not busy," Nezha replied quickly.

Salwa smiled.

"Are you interested in making ten thousand dirhams, which equals a million centimes?"

The word "a million" had an amazing ring for Nezha. The amount was so large she couldn't wrap her head around it. She thought Salwa might be teasing her.

"Yeah, I want to make a million centimes. What do I have to do?"

"If you can promise me that you are still a virgin, come back tomorrow at noon."

Nezha thought about her encounters with her teacher. He was careful to keep things tame so as not to risk taking her virginity.

"Are you still a virgin?" Salwa asked.

Nezha blushed. "I'm a virgin," she replied, feeling compelled to respond.

Salwa explained that the ten thousand dirhams would be for the cost of her virginity.

The next day, Nezha returned to the salon a little before noon. Salwa opened the door for her, greeting her with a kiss on both cheeks. She gestured for Nezha to take a seat on the sofa.

A few minutes after Nezha's arrival, a woman with a mouthful of gold teeth entered the salon. She was veiled and spoke in a Marrakesh accent. She immediately walked over to Nezha and inspected her carefully. Nezha was nervous and quiet while she waited for the woman to finish looking her over.

"Do whatever this woman tells you, like she's your mother," Salwa instructed.

The woman took Nezha by the hand and led her to a cab that was waiting outside. The cab dropped them off at a luxurious villa in one of the most upscale neighborhoods in Casablanca, called California. Nezha was wide-eyed as she took in the extravagant mansion. The woman headed toward the door, leading Nezha by the hand. She rang the doorbell and a burly guard wearing a tracksuit and holding a huge club in one hand opened the door. He smiled at the woman and quickly glanced at Nezha, and then gestured for them to follow him.

The garden extended as far as the eye could see and was edged with leafy shrubs and exquisite rosebushes. Nezha absorbed the fragrances and colors of the garden as the guard and woman led her to a shaded area at the far end of the garden, an oasis from the hot afternoon sun. The woman took a seat at the table, clearly familiar with her surroundings, and waited for a moment to let Nezha take in the full grandeur of the garden.

"Everything will go well," she said, taking Nezha by the hand and smiling at her. "The sheikh is decent and generous. He won't hurt you. Had I known fate would have us cross paths, I would have given him twenty girls."

Nezha didn't really understand what the woman meant, but she felt safe inside this magical place and smiled to show her appreciation.

"Salwa didn't explain what I'm supposed to do."

"There isn't anything that needs to be explained. Everything will go smoothly as long as you're a virgin. It's so hard to find virgins your age these days. I don't know when things changed, but girls these days are sinful. How old are you?"

"Sixteen."

"Are you an orphan?"

"Well, my dad died not long ago."

"Right, that's what Salwa said. I like to help kids who have lost a parent since I raised my kids on my own. Listen, if you're obedient—and it seems you are—I'll introduce you to some very important people and you won't have to worry about anything ever again, inshallah."

Nezha didn't know if she was supposed to thank this woman or not, so she just nodded and waited for whatever was in store for her.

The housekeeper approached them and gave a cursory greeting, barely even looking at them. The woman promptly stood and nudged Nezha forward.

"You can leave now," the housekeeper said coldly to the woman who had brought Nezha.

The woman nodded and retreated toward a side door, where the guard was standing. He pointed with his club to a car parked near the walkway.

"Wait in the car," he said. "The driver will bring you back when it's time."

The housekeeper took Nezha by the hand and brought her into a splendid parlor filled with elegant divans. She left Nezha standing there, without instructing her to sit down, and then disappeared through a small door. This is a real palace, Nezha thought to herself, as she stared at the ornate ceiling, the glistening chandeliers, and delicate antiques. She waited there for over two hours.

The housekeeper returned, and with a cold expression grabbed Nezha tightly by the hand and led her to a small door with a golden handle. When she opened it, Nezha found herself in a large bedroom with what looked to be a comfortable bed, sofas, a large dresser, and several chairs. The sheikh was sitting on one of the massive, tufted sofas. He looked over seventy, wore tinted black glasses, and was dressed in the finest Gulfie robes. Nezha suddenly realized that she was alone in the room with him. She hadn't noticed the housekeeper slip out. The sheikh was deep in thought, focused solely on the prayer beads in his hand. She could hear him mutter fragments of prayers, the words unintelligibly meshed together in repetition. He seemed not to notice Nezha until he had finished his recitation. He kissed the beads and placed them under a pillow.

"Come closer, my girl. Come closer," he said, motioning to a spot beside him.

It was at this moment that she realized he was blind. She drew closer, taking short, cautious steps until she stood in front of him. He extended his hand to touch her and she froze.

"A bit closer. Don't be afraid."

When she edged even closer, he took hold of her and sat her down on the chair facing him. He began touching her face lightly, reading her features with his palms and then gently tracing the shape of her nose and mouth with his fingertip. Nezha was waiting for him to start groping her chest, and down below.

"How old are you?" he asked.

"Sixteen."

He nodded, satisfied, and then placed his hand on her knee. "Did they tell you what you have to do?"

"What do I have to do?" she asked, her voice hoarse.

"Take your clothes off over there," he said, pointing to a door in the corner that led to another room, "then clean up and put on the white pajamas."

After a brief hesitation she headed to the room, feeling confused, and still not exactly sure what she was being asked to do. She returned to the bedroom wearing the white pajamas, feeling like a patient in a hospital. She found the sheikh still seated on the sofa, but he had taken off his robes and was in his undergarments. His old, wrinkled body disgusted her and she hoped to get this finished quickly, get her ten thousand dirhams, and then forget it all. He asked her to sit in front of him, and removed his black-tinted glasses. She had never seen eyes like his before—dark, glassy, and hideous. She had to look away to keep from feeling nauseated.

"Take off your pajamas and open your legs, my girl," he said with a fatherly sweetness.

Nezha paused for a second and looked closely at his face—maybe she'd discover a kind soul behind this ugly façade, but she couldn't bear to look for long. She was terrified of him. She hurriedly removed her pajamas, and sat in her underwear. She reached out to touch him to let him know that she was ready. She had no idea how he planned to have sex with her. She was hoping he would bring her to the bed—maybe that would be quicker and gentler. Instead, he grabbed her thighs like he was inspecting cattle. His hands climbed up until he reached her underwear, which he took off gently. Then he told her to relax and open her legs. She was scared as first, but remembered that he was blind. Why wouldn't he just bring her to the comfortable bed? Did he want something other than sex? The way he was situated in front of her didn't seem relaxing or indicative of some sexual position; rather, it was like she was at the women's clinic. Her confusion only increased when he touched her vagina without flinching or showing any signs of satisfaction. He began by inserting one finger, gently and determinedly, like he was used to doing this. She felt his finger enter her, and didn't know how to react. She watched his hideous face contort with displeasure as he probed inside her. She felt his fingernail scratch her, causing her to pull back in pain. He scolded her, using words she didn't understand. Then he inserted his entire finger, and when he withdrew it, it was smeared with blood. He raised his finger to his eyes and began wiping his eyelids with her blood.

The sudden silence of the hair dryer being turned off brought Nezha back to reality. She couldn't quite catch her breath and tried not to cry. She felt Salwa pat her on the shoulder.

"You haven't even checked out your hair. Do you like this do?"

"Sorry, Salwa, I was thinking about that horrible experience with the sheikh."

Salwa bit her lip, dropped her shoulders, and sighed. "You're still thinking about that, after all this time? I bet you've experienced worse since."

Nezha nodded. "You're right. My life has been a series of trials, tribulations, and suffering. What reminded me of the sheikh was what happened yesterday with Hamadi—in both instances I made out horribly. Yesterday, I got nothing. With the sheikh, I only got a thousand dirhams instead of the ten thousand promised."

Salwa tried to keep quiet, knowing that Nezha hadn't really processed what happened.

"Listen, the mistake was yours. You were the one who lied when you said you were a virgin."

"But I *was* a virgin! I promised you that my only experience was with that teacher and it was nothing. He never penetrated me. And the sheikh, he smeared his eyes with my blood. If I wasn't a virgin then he wouldn't have gotten a single drop."

Salwa stared at her through the mirror and leaned over. "He didn't think you were a virgin, my dear. What came out was just the very last bit of your virginity. The sheikh is an expert in these things. I hope he is cured of his blindness. He's violated hundreds of girls to no avail."

"God will take revenge on everyone who stole my honor," Nezha said, looking up at the ceiling.

Salwa gave her an angry look. "I know that you still think we took your money—how many times have I sworn on the holy book . . ."

"That's not important," Nezha interrupted. "What's important is this: can you lend me some money now?"

Salwa reached for the pack of cigarettes on top of the counter, lit one, and exhaled the smoke in short bursts, thinking about how many little loans Nezha never repaid. And Nezha always preceded her request with this same memory.

"If you need something like fifty dirhams, no problem, but I don't have more than that."

Nezha spun around in the styling chair, turning her back to the mirror. "I need two thousand at least. I need to give Farqash half of that or he'll kill me. The other half is for household expenses. Just give me a month, at most, and I promise you both your money and something special."

Salwa nearly said no immediately, but chose to decline gently instead. "I swear to God, my dear—and here's my bag, check it yourself—I am suffering financially because of these religious zealots. Most girls are now veiled and no longer need a salon, so I'm thinking about selling it. And I'm scared one of these guys will blow himself up in here."

Nezha reached for the cigarettes and lit one. As she exhaled, her stomach rumbled and she felt sick. Except for the cup of black coffee, she hadn't had anything to eat or drink since yesterday morning. Salwa walked over to the counter and began arranging her hairstyling equipment, making it clear that she was done with Nezha.

5

Nezha left Salwa's Salon fuming. She took a deep breath and headed in the direction of the bus station, a place she detested. It had been ages since she'd taken the bus. She had the mobile numbers of a handful of cab drivers who would drop everything, no matter where they were or who they were driving, to come pick her up when she called. But at that moment, she couldn't indulge in this luxury. Salwa had only given her fifty dirhams, which was about enough for a pack of cigarettes and a bus ticket. As she stood there waiting for the next bus, she thought about what a terrible situation she was in. She was alone and afraid, with no one to protect her.

She fought back tears as she thought about her father. Despite his financial troubles and sickness he had always been there to provide her with love and support. He had sacrificed so much to give her what she wanted, however meager it was. She closed her eyes and pictured her father with his gentle, ever-present smile. She remembered how he would take her by the hand, stroke her hair, and embrace her lovingly. She thought about all the men she had been with since who had never really cared for her. Their hearts beat with cruelty.

She got worked up recalling these memories. As she tried to catch her breath she suddenly noticed her brother standing in front of the station. Was he spying on her? She looked at him suspiciously. Why was he wearing sports gear? He only wore those clothes when he went out jogging with friends. Why was he wearing the cap that he used to cover his face when he pretended to be sleeping? She squinted at him, examining his appearance as he crossed the street and walked toward her. As he approached, people waiting at the station turned to look at him. He was agitated and looked as if he were ready to pounce on her. She pulled back as he reached for her arm.

"What do you want from me?" she said in a loud voice, drawing the attention of those around her.

He stared at the onlookers who were now surrounding them, as if he were ready to take on each and every one of them.

"Where are you going?" he said through his clenched jaw.

"It's none of your business where I'm going," she said coldly.

She moved away, but he stayed close.

"You humiliated me in front of my friends—"

"You and your friends," she interrupted, "do absolutely nothing except keep tabs on everyone else. All you do is stand around and gossip like women! Why don't you look for jobs? If you don't like the fact that I have a job, why don't you go get one yourself! I'd love to stay home. I could use a break."

She didn't know where this courage and strength sprang from inside her. She noticed her brother's irritation. He looked around, scared that some nosy passerby might have caught what she said.

"If I *could* find a job, I wouldn't be standing here," he said, trying to maintain his composure.

"Leave me alone, for our mother's sake," she said. "Or do you want her back in a hospital bed again?"

Ibrahim looked at his sister in disbelief, his anger intensifying. "You talk about your job like you're some respectable employee."

"I *am* a respectable employee," she said firmly.

"Where do you work?"

"None of your business."

"If your job is respectable then let me come along."

She shook her head. "I'm not working tonight, but if you want to join me tomorrow, be my guest."

"Where are you going now?" he asked.

"To a friend's place."

She backed away a few paces, but he closed in again. She was scared he was about to lash out, but instead a strange smile spread over his face.

"You were at Salwa's Salon," he said, leaning into her ear. "The bus you're waiting for is headed downtown— what's downtown except cafés, bars, and whorehouses? Do you think I don't know what you do? Do you think I'm really asleep when you return drunk, smelling like cigarettes and beer? I've defended your reputation nearly every single day. I've been ready to fight anyone who has even thought about attacking you. You'll never be able to understand how much I've suffered on your behalf. But yesterday, when they saw you get out of that car like that, you exposed it all. Your cover was blown."

"What happened yesterday will never happen again, I promise you."

He grabbed her arm so hard that she nearly screamed. He no longer cared what everyone around them thought.

"Come back to the house with me."

She freed her arm from his clutch and looked at him. She could see sparks flying in his eyes.

"Get away from me!" she yelled. "Who are you? I don't know you!"

Ibrahim froze in place, looking at her in disbelief. His heart raced and he could feel the blood rush into his face. He stood there mortified and could hear murmurs in support of Nezha. From the corner of his eye he saw a guy move forward as if he were about to intervene.

Nezha couldn't understand exactly how she lost control, and how all this anger erupted. Her face went white, she started breathing heavily, and her limbs shook. Everyone watching assumed the situation was about to get worse. Then the bus pulled in slowly. Just before it stopped, Nezha caught a glimpse of Sufyan and Driss, who had been keeping an eye on the altercation from the other side of the street.

*

In the Ain Seba industrial area east of Casablanca there was a
factory that specialized in manufacturing electrical cables for
vehicles. The company was owned by a giant German cor-
poration, which, like many corporations, preferred the lower
labor costs and special tax deductions in Morocco, not to
mention its proximity to Europe for easy export.

The factory had a typical assembly line where all of
the workers, men and women alike, stood in their assigned
place, adding their own little segment to the cable before it
moved along the line to the next person. No one, no matter
what, could leave their workstation or make a single mistake for fear of jamming the line and shutting down the
machines, resulting in hours of repairs. In classic German
style, the workers moved quickly, but with precision. Despite
the physicality of the job, the workers were thankful that at
least the machines were quiet—allowing them to chat with
one another all day.

This week had been particularly grueling. The workers
weren't allowed to take any time off and worked extra hours
for a rush order from a big contractor in Europe. As com-
pensation, the company promised everyone an extra day's
holiday. Abdel-Jalil and Said, two of the employees, eagerly
awaited the sound of the bell as they approached the last
fifteen minutes of their shift. They were antsy. Not only were
they in the first group to be given the following day off, but
today was payday, and it included all of the overtime they

had worked this month. Abdel-Jalil and Said had become close friends working together on the line. They were both overqualified for their positions—one had a university degree in physics, the other a degree in environmental science—but the lack of job opportunities in the country pushed them to employment that didn't make use of their skills. That said, they were actually among the fortunate—at least they were able to get jobs in this factory.

They stood next to one another, their hands moving quickly. The monotony of the day had taken its toll. They looked haggard and ached to get off of their feet. They had discussed every topic imaginable and had nothing more to talk about except what they would do when they finished their shift—but the minutes were dragging.

"I've changed my mind," said Said, without shifting his eyes from the workstation. "I'm not going to go with you to Fez. I'm not leaving my house. What I want, need, and dream of, is to relax and just sleep."

Said was thirty, just like his friend. He had a large white mark around his right temple that drew stares and made him feel undesirable. As a result, he was cynical and antagonistic toward most people. Quite the opposite of Said, Abdel-Jalil was a likable guy. He was handsome, and always well dressed and clean-shaven.

"Why have you changed your mind so quickly?" Abdel-Jalil asked, disappointed.

Said didn't answer his friend's question.

"I'm tired too," Abdel-Jalil added, sighing. "I don't want to travel, but it's the first of the month. I have to visit my family and give them some money."

"Send them a money transfer like last month and apologize over the phone. Tell them we don't have a break."

"I promised them I'd visit. Also, I miss my mother and siblings."

Said was the one who sighed this time, loudly, more like a groan, as he closed his eyes for a moment. He thought about the cold, family-less world he inhabited. His mother had divorced his father years ago and married another man. His one sister lived in Spain with her husband and children.

Abdel-Jalil sensed that his friend Said was deep in thought, which was his usual response when they had this conversation.

"What do you think about having dinner at our friend Baaroub's restaurant?" he asked to lighten the mood. "Then I'll head home to pack up some stuff, go get a ticket at the station, and come to your place and hang out until I need to leave."

Said cheered up at this suggestion. The assembly line came to a stop and the bell rang marking the end of their shift. The workers swarmed to the exits of the building like they were running from a fire. They all lined up in front of the cashier to get their wages.

Baaroub's restaurant was one of the most popular local joints downtown. It served up traditional Moroccan dishes, like tagines and kebabs, with a modern flair. They were known for their harira soup and maaqouda, a simple dish of fried potatoes, spices, and eggs. The friends each placed an order of both dishes. They sat at their favorite table in the corner, eating and chatting away. At a neighboring table sat a young man and a pretty, elegant girl, who kept laughing as she ate. The way the couple was positioned, Said was facing her, and whenever they looked at one another Said was struck with envy.

"I'd love to meet a cheerful girl like her."

Abdel-Jalil turned around to check her out. He thought she was ordinary and unattractive. Abdel-Jalil knew that watching this couple was eating away at Said. Most women found Said unsightly and he had given up on trying to find one to marry.

"Do you think you're the only one who wants to get married?" Abdel-Jalil asked to distract him. "I want to get married too, but I can't seem to find anyone either."

Said put down his food, feeling even more drawn to the girl across from him. "If I met a girl who liked me," he said, "it wouldn't be complicated. I'd recite the opening verses of the Quran and marry her on the spot."

Abdel-Jalil finished his harira and chomped down on the last big piece of maaqouda. "We've said the same thing a thousand times," he said.

"The next time will be different," Said replied energetically. "As soon as I find a girl who likes me I'm going to propose on the spot. I'll tell her directly: 'Allow me to introduce myself. My name is Said. I'm thirty years old. I live in a decent place downtown, even though it's a bit small and old. I work at a factory that produces electrical cables and I make three thousand dirhams a month. I'm a serious and reasonable guy. Will you marry me?' If she said yes, we'd get engaged that same day, without a moment's hesitation. I wouldn't ask her about her past, who she is, what she owns, whether she works or not."

Abdel-Jalil smiled, hoping to add a bit of levity to this tedious conversation that Said never seemed to tire of discussing.

"It's like you bought a watermelon and you have no idea whether it's sweet inside until you open it," Abdel-Jalil joked.

The girl at the other table laughed loudly, almost as if she were mocking their ridiculous conversation. Said took this gesture personally and sank down further in his chair, as if the girl's laugh had intentionally wounded him. He looked up to shoot her a nasty look, but she was already absorbed in conversation with her male companion. She was listening to him intently, and he seemed to be telling her a fascinating story.

"Don't pay attention to her," Abdel-Jalil said, snapping Said out of it.

Said shuddered like someone pulled away from watching an intense movie.

"Let's go," Said said. "On to our misery."

Abdel-Jalil paid the bill as Said got a final look at the two lovers, who seemed to be in another world altogether.

*

Nezha rushed onto the bus as soon as it stopped at the station. She squeezed her way through the crowd, which was crammed like a can of sardines. She told herself: "If I don't turn around, I won't see what's behind me. Stay calm. Don't be afraid."

Every time the bus stopped and passengers got off Nezha would act as if she were moving toward the front door, to see if anyone would follow her if she got up. She wasn't sure if her brother or one of his friends had boarded as well. She was frightened, and was ready to bolt from the bus at any moment. As they approached the intersection with the busiest downtown street, the signal turned red. The bus stopped in the middle of a line of cars. Nezha stood and shuffled to the front, getting so close to the bus driver that he was forced to look at her. When he looked up she leaned in toward his ear and whispered: "Maybe you could let me off here?"

"Why not, beautiful?"

He pressed the button to open the door and Nezha slipped out before the door had fully opened. She made her way through the cars and then darted into a side street teeming with pedestrians. She smiled victoriously and said to herself: "Nezha can do it all!" Then, catching herself being cocky, she apologized: "Forgive me, Lord." She passed a number of buildings before branching off into an empty alleyway, constantly checking behind her. She walked under the pale light of the streetlamps, passing the back doors of cafés, hotels, and bars. It was a warm night, like those November nights that increasingly seemed to be an extension of the summer during these years of drought.

By the time Nezha approached the back door of La Falaise she was strutting and feeling a bit bolder. "Whatever happens, happens," she said to herself as she climbed the narrow, unlit back stairs. She found herself in the dressing room. It was empty and smelled of a mixture of cheap perfume and sweat. The floor was littered with used tissues. Nezha stared at herself in the mirror. She picked up one of the lipsticks from the counter in front of her and started painting the deep red onto her lips. She paused, leaning in to look at her reflection and questioning her decision to come here.

She entered the bar and found it empty except for a few girls she vaguely knew, who were flirting with customers. She froze when she saw Farqash at the bar with Warda. She watched as he lit her cigarette and caressed her hand. He wrapped his arm around her waist, drew her close, and kissed her. Nezha walked over to the booth closest to them and sat down. She slammed down her pack of cigarettes.

"Warda, one beer over here!" she shouted, intent on disrupting their embrace.

Farqash turned toward her in disbelief. Warda froze, awaiting Farqash's instructions. Without even looking at her he shook his head, telling Warda not to bring her a beer, and walked toward Nezha. He grabbed a chair and sat in front of her.

"You have my money?" he asked in a threatening tone.

"I know you're aware of what happened last night."

Farqash gnashed his big, yellowed teeth, grumbled, and slammed his fist on the table. "Listen, you whore, I don't care about your life story. If you don't put the money on this table, I'll wipe you off the face of this planet." As he spoke his nostrils flared like a bull's, filled with rage toward her.

Nezha thought about how everything in her life had gone downhill the day Salwa introduced her to this animal. Salwa had presented him to Nezha as her protector, as someone who would look after her. At the time, Nezha had no idea how the nightlife operated. Farqash had masterminded their whole relationship. He claimed her as his favorite and made her feel like the princess of La Falaise. He helped her earn a lot of money, taught her how to smoke, drink, and flirt like a professional. But once he'd gained control over her he began punishing her for any little slipup, no matter how trivial. He would beat her with his belt and throw things at her. One time, when she refused to have anal sex with him, he hit her on the head with a bottle, resulting in a cut so deep that she still had the scar. Another time he raped her so aggressively that she was left bedridden for a week. From that day on, he instilled such fear in her that she would do anything he asked, without resistance or delay. She knew he would be brutal with her if she made him mad, but he was so moody that it became difficult to predict when he would have one of his outbursts.

One night, when he was drunk, he confided that he had killed a man. He opened a case underneath his bed and showed her a long shiny sword. She thought he was going to kill her on the spot. But he satisfied himself with beating her instead, and warned her that he was watching her. He said he knew about her attempts to flee and work at other clubs. He warned her that all the other club owners in Casablanca were his friends, and no matter what she did, she'd never be able to escape. He reminded her of some of the girls with disfigured faces who begged for cigarettes and pennies outside the clubs. He told her they'd been just like her, but had disobeyed or tried to scam him. He reminded her of Farida, his most recent victim: she would put a hand over the top of her mouth to hide the nasty scar that made her smile from ear to ear like a menacing clown. After midnight Farida would be outside, begging for cigarettes or money to buy a bottle of cheap liquor from her old friends.

All the other girls in the bar constantly flattered Nezha and gave her fancy cigarettes and gifts, in hopes that if Farqash got mad at one of them, Nezha might intervene on her behalf. Her happiest days were when Farqash spoiled her, embraced her, and slapped her ass. She never thought that Warda's presence would change things so quickly. Warda, that fat-assed Bedouin, was now sitting on the throne. She hated hearing the other women calling Warda's name instead of hers. When Nezha first complained to Farqash that he wasn't paying as much attention to her, he beat her brutally. To make his point, he took out his sword, placed the blade on her neck, and made it clear what would happen if she complained again. Farqash quickly changed all the rules, and started demanding that Nezha make a nightly payment to him, just like all the other girls. One night she picked a fight with Warda, who proved to be just as vicious as Farqash. She started thinking of leaving, but where would she go? As long as she was in demand at La Falaise, she wasn't allowed to work anywhere else.

In the end, she gave in to her new reality. To cope, she started drinking more. She didn't turn down a single request. She placed no boundaries on what she was willing to do with men. What does it matter what they do to me? she thought. Farqash would do the same or worse. Just when she thought that Farqash would stop making demands, he surprised her by insisting on a huge cut from her recent outings with Hamadi. He started threatening to kill her if wasn't paid his fair share.

Now, sitting across from her, he was looking at her in disbelief. He was put off by her calmness as she took a cigarette out of the pack. She lit it, took a long, slow drag, and exhaled right into his face.

"I ordered a beer. Didn't you hear me?" she shouted, looking past Farqash at Warda.

Warda remained frozen in place. The other patrons started to quiet down and look in their direction, sensing the tension between the three.

"Nezha is making a huge mistake," Warda said to a client nearby. "She thinks she still holds sway in this place, but she's dreaming, and these dreams are going to get her killed."

"She's just a whore," replied the client, stammering in a drunken stupor. "Whores don't have dreams."

Nezha was determined to order a beer, as if her life depended on it. But Warda shot her a nasty look and turned to help other patrons.

"You're ignoring me?" she shouted, jumping to her feet. "The Bedouin of La Falaise! Oh, don't worry, your day will come, my dear."

Farqash grabbed Nezha's hand and squeezed it in his fist, nearly breaking her fingers.

"Get the hell out of here," he said between his teeth, trying to control his anger. "I know exactly when I'm going to punish you for causing this scene."

Nezha didn't pay attention to his threat. She didn't even feel her hand being crushed, as if it were numb. For the first time, she stood up to his intimidation.

"If you are a man, punish me right now!" she said, challenging him. "You're an evil, controlling bastard who preys on the weak like me. What are you waiting for?"

Was it even thinkable to insult this man? Was this really Nezha the coward saying these things directly to Casablanca's most dangerous pimp? It couldn't really be her. Everyone thought that she must be high, must be on something really strong. But the truth was, she was high on the horrible memories of her life, which were running like a film reel in front of her. All she could see were scenes of humiliation, insult, fear, and the people who had so cruelly taken advantage of her.

Farqash, shocked, looked her over carefully, unable to figure out what was going on. Nezha stared back defiantly, and he couldn't say anything. The entire place was waiting on his next move, holding their breath.

He changed course, and leaned toward her, speaking in a soft, unthreatening tone, as if he were going to come to a friendly compromise with her. "I'm going to kill you tonight. And when they take your body to the morgue to do the autopsy, they are going to find that beer bottle you requested, jammed inside."

Nezha burst out laughing, as if she'd just heard a hilarious joke. "Life doesn't matter to me any more, you bastard. What matters is embarrassing you in front of everyone." She looked around and started back in on him. "This bastard takes advantage of weak women. He steals their hard-earned money. If one of us makes a hundred dirhams, he takes fifty— and if we sell our bodies elsewhere, we still have to pay him. He prohibits us from working at other clubs. He's a pervert who likes anal, and he deals coke too. He even admitted to me that he killed someone . . ."

Farqash's heart started pounding, his breathing quickened, and his fists clenched. He tried to resist the urge to pound them into Nezha's face. He didn't care what she said about him, but he wouldn't have his name dragged through the mud by this whore. He stood up, shaking with anger, and gestured to Warda, indicating that she turn up the music. As the song got louder, Nezha's voice could no longer be heard.

She didn't know what would happen next; all she wanted was a cold beer. She headed to the counter where Warda stood.

"Give me a beer, Warda," she said. "This is my last request in life."

Warda looked at her with confusion and pity. She nearly carried out her request, but Farqash motioned to her, stopping her from reaching for a glass. Warda nodded, understanding his message, and drifted back toward the corner.

"Please, Warda," Nezha said, looking at her imploringly. "One beer and I'll head out."

Warda looked at her, still confused. She was searching for an excuse to help her, as she started to realize that Nezha's behavior might not be the result of being high on some drug. Farqash recognized what was going on inside Warda's head. He moved to the counter, grabbed Nezha by the arm, dragged her to the door, and kicked her out as if she were a small dog.

Nezha found herself out on the street, hungry, disoriented, and penniless. She started walking. She had conquered her fear and exploded right in Farqash's face—this was what she had long dreamed of doing. Now she was free, and if Farqash tried to control her again, she'd go straight to Detective Hanash and tell him everything she knew. She had enough information to send Farqash to jail for the rest of his life.

She lit a cigarette, inhaled deeply, and lifted her face to the sky, letting the smoke circle her head. She burned down half the cigarette in three drags and threw the remaining half on the ground, stamping it out with her foot. A few steps later she emerged from the alley and was on Mohamed V Street, the biggest street in Casablanca. "Now I'm free," she told herself, "and whatever comes will come."

The bus station wasn't very busy at this hour. Abdel-Jalil headed toward the ticket window with the sign for Fez and waited until the woman in front of him finished. He checked out her prominent ass before she left her spot at the counter.

"One ticket on the midnight bus to Fez, please."

The employee at the counter handed him the ticket. "Want to know the seat number of the woman with the nice ass just before you? Number twelve."

Abdel-Jalil looked at his ticket, and his eyes widened. "And you gave me seat number thirteen."

"You're gonna have the best trip of your life," the elderly ticket man said sarcastically.

Abdel-Jalil left the station quickly, hoping he might spot the woman. Who knows, maybe she was by herself and didn't have anything to do for the next four hours until the bus left. He raced out the door and looked in all directions. He cursed himself for not paying more attention to her when they were in line. He tried to recall what she looked like. He didn't have a clear picture of her in his mind, having seen her from behind and been more focused on her ass than anything else. He had a feeling that she was middle-aged, wore a traditional jalabiya, and her hair was covered. Maybe she was more the type of the old employee.

Abdel-Jalil didn't feel like heading back to the cold apartment. He had everything he needed in his jacket pockets. He wouldn't be staying in Fez for more than a day, and he had clothes, pajamas, and shaving supplies there. He always preferred to travel without bags—it made him feel free. As he headed downtown he thought about when he had first come to Casablanca three years ago, after one of his cousins had gotten him the job at the factory. At the time, Abdel-Jalil was so disappointed because he was hoping for a more stable government position in the public works department.

He felt overqualified and out of place at work, and this always gave him the sense that his situation was temporary. Like other well-educated guys, he dreamed of emigrating to Canada, and he participated in the US visa lottery every year. He had looked into emigrating to Europe, whether legally with a job offer, or as a "harrag," hiding away on a boat.

He had grown up in a poor but close-knit family. His father made ceramics and had a small shop where he sold clay pots. There wasn't much demand for ceramics these days and there was a lot of competition, making it difficult for his father to earn a steady income. His mother was a housewife who spent her time doing the seemingly endless household chores. Abdel-Jalil had the nickname "the Sisters' Brother," since he had three sisters, all of whom still lived in the same rundown home in Fez's Old City with their parents. The sisters were all on the path to becoming spinsters. Abdel-Jalil, at thirty, was the youngest sibling. He felt a deep responsibility to help his family, despite his meager monthly wages. And now he had a thousand dirhams for all the extra hours he had put in at the factory.

He fingered the bills in his jacket pocket as he strutted down the street dressed in his best clothes. He had combed his hair back and put on cologne, and looked suave. As he walked he was overcome with a sense of ease and satisfaction. He decided to just enjoy taking a stroll on Mohamed V Street. He wouldn't think about the past or the future; he'd just live in the moment.

Abdel-Jalil walked down the sidewalk with his hands in his pockets, whistling and checking out the women passing by. He stopped in his tracks in disbelief the moment he saw Nezha. She seemed to be in a daze, as if she were in another world. He looked at her and rushed toward her.

"Is it you?" he asked.

He moved in and planted two warm kisses on her cheeks. Nezha had still not come to her senses, and was about to reply impolitely, "No, I'm not who you think."

But instead she inspected him, noticing how attractive he was, and the scent of his lovely cologne. She was a bit overwhelmed by this man's good looks and his chipper mood. Then it hit her—she remembered the last time she had slept with him, about two months ago. She felt at ease, remembering that this guy, despite being a bit stingy—he'd never given her more than a hundred dirhams—always made her feel comfortable, and she liked spending time with him. She looked around, scared that there was someone on her tracks.

"Where have you been all this time?" she asked.

"I went to La Falaise one other time, but you were busy."

She laughed. "My time there is over," she said decisively. "I'm a free agent now. It's probably best if you stop going there. If I told you what they do to their customers, you'd never set foot in there again. They're all crooks."

"I'm not a customer," he interrupted. "When I used to go to La Falaise, it was to find you. Anyway, where are you going now?"

Nezha hesitated for a moment. What she really needed was to forget about Farqash and the problems with her brother. She felt that what she wanted right now was to get wasted and pass out. She looked up at Abdel-Jalil and was pleased to see that he was practically drooling over her.

"You're looking sharp," she said. "Do you have a date?"

"I'm heading to Fez on the midnight bus to visit my family."

This response shattered her hopes. She stepped back a bit, visibly losing interest in him.

"I'll see you when you get back, then," she said, disappointed.

He seized her by the shoulders and drew her closer, his face full of lust. "I want to see you now."

Nezha looked into his eyes and gave a coy smile, fluttering her fingers on his palm to cajole him. "Didn't you say that you're traveling to Fez at midnight?"

He took Nezha by the hand as if she would escape and swiftly looked at his watch. "I still have more than four hours," he said.

He looked at her hopefully, and Nezha read the plea in his eyes. She knew exactly what this look meant in a situation like this: he was so riled up he would drop anything to get laid.

"What can we do in four hours?" she teased him. She had him in the palm of her hand.

"We can do everything in four hours. We won't waste any time going to my house, which is too far away. Let's go to my friend's house. It's really close."

"There's no way I'm going to your friend's house," she said decisively. Her refusal was firm. Experience had taught her that being alone with two friends ended in one of two outcomes: a fight, or they would try to have a threesome with her. "If you want me to join you for a beer at some bar, I'm up for it, but let's leave the other things for when you get back from Fez. You have my number—call whenever you want."

Abdel-Jalil drew her close again. "I suggested my friend's place only to save a bit of time. But if you want to go to my house, no problem. Let's take a cab."

He stepped out to hail a cab, but Nezha stopped him. She knew that Abdel-Jalil's house was way out on another side of Casablanca, and the cab fare there and back would be costly, and this would affect what he paid her. She reconsidered, thinking that everything would happen pretty quickly: he'd have sex with her and then drop her off on the corner.

"All right, I'll go to your friend's house. But you have to give me five hundred dirhams now, like a down payment."

He went silent. This request embarrassed him. She knew he was just a factory employee. Even when he went to La Falaise once a month he'd arrive drunk so he only had to pay for a beer or two, while sitting alone for hours. Despite knowing this, she expected him to respond differently this time, since it was no longer his head making the decisions.

"I'll give you a hundred dirhams in advance," he said, imagining the amount of pleasure that awaited him.

She laughed deeply, thinking that this amount, were he someone else, wouldn't even cover the cost of the cigarettes she smoked for the evening. But she gave in. Her plan was to head to a bar far from downtown after she left Abdel-Jalil. She'd keep drinking there, and find someone to take her on an adventure.

He led Nezha from Mohamed V down one of the alleys that took them right in front of La Falaise. He said it was the easiest way to get to his friend Said's house, and Nezha didn't protest. She was actually looking forward to bravely walking by the place.

"You know that my house is far from downtown. Plus, the neighborhood is full of nosy people. Here, the streets are empty and people mind their own business."

That certainly wasn't how Nezha viewed this neighborhood. She imagined a group of people watching and following them. When she dared look back, her mouth suddenly dry, she only saw random people crossing the street. When they reached the grimiest section of the street, Abdel-Jalil twisted into a narrow, dark alley.

"Here's Said's place," he said, invigorated.

The apartment building was ancient and nearly collapsing. On the wall was a hand-painted sign: "No Urinating." Despite this, a powerful, pungent smell of urine hit them from the corner. The building's door was made of rickety wood. The stairway was unlit, so Abdel-Jalil had to use his lighter to lead the way. Nezha stayed close, as she felt the floor shift under her feet. Abdel-Jalil smiled at her, assuring her that he knew his way.

"Don't be afraid. This building is from the days of the Roman Empire," he joked. "Even though it moves around a bit, it's stronger than the structures they build today. My friend Said is lucky because the monthly rent is really low."

Nezha didn't offer a reply, and when Abdel-Jalil extinguished his lighter she felt as if she were inside a coffin. He knocked on the door, and as soon as it opened light poured into the entryway. Nezha caught her breath and hurried inside.

The apartment was small but, in contrast to the state of the entryway, was quite beautiful and classy. The living room contained a sofa, chairs, and an elegant coffee table with an, albeit cracked, glass top. It was clear that the furniture was used. Nezha looked around, scanning the place, not even paying attention to its occupant, until Abdel-Jalil introduced his friend.

"This is my friend . . . well, my brother, Said. And this is Nezha."

Nezha's eyes went directly to the mark around Said's temple. She noted how unattractive he was in comparison to his friend, but didn't let that stop her from greeting him warmly, like she'd known him for ages. He rushed toward her and kissed her on each cheek, in awe as he inspected her from top to bottom, unable to restrain himself. A look of total fascination spread over his face, as if he'd seen something miraculous. Then he started moving around her, devouring her with his eyes, like a raging bull. Nezha looked straight back at him and mimicked his movements, laughing. Abdel-Jalil was getting annoyed with all this back-and-forth. He scanned the room, noticed a bottle of red wine that was nearly empty, and realized that Said was drunk. He tried to control his anger.

"You took down a bottle of red that quickly?" Abdel-Jalil said with a smile, mildly reproaching him. "Didn't you say that you only wanted to catch up on sleep?"

Said didn't pay attention to his friend. Instead, he got closer to Nezha, nearly touching her.

"Welcome, Nezha, to my home," he said, cheerfully. "Let me show you around."

He took her hand and led her to the bedroom. It was small, but very clean. It had a comfortable-looking bed and a new armoire, and the floor was covered with a thick red carpet, like a hotel room.

On one of the bedside tables Nezha saw an open envelope brimming with cash. She couldn't keep her eyes off the envelope. If only I had that money, all my problems would be solved, she thought to herself. Said stepped away from her to grab the envelope and secure the cash inside it, and then shoved it into a drawer. He then took her by the arm and led her to another corner of the apartment, which was set up as the kitchen, and finally showed her where the bathroom was. When they returned to the living room they were both laughing and giggling.

Said looked at Abdel-Jalil, who had sunk into the couch. He had a hand on his cheek, unable to hide his frown.

"Don't worry about him," Said said to Nezha. "You're a guest in my home. What would you like to drink, sweetheart?"

Nezha laughed, feeling like all of her troubles had washed away. After seeing the envelope full of cash in the bedroom and hearing him use the word *sweetheart*, she felt like she was floating on a cloud.

"What do you have to drink?" she asked.

Said moved in closer, stumbling a bit. "The refrigerator is full to the brim! I've got everything your heart desires."

"What are we waiting for, then? Let's drink! I'm dying of thirst," she said, beaming with excitement.

Said let out a resounding laugh, but instead of heading to the kitchen he threw himself on the couch. "Hey Abdel-Jalil, my home is your home—you know where the fridge is."

Abdel-Jalil hesitated, fighting back his irritation. He got up and headed to the fridge. As soon as he disappeared, Said lit a cigarette and offered one to Nezha. When she leaned in to get a light, he yanked her closer and sat her down next to him. She took a long drag and exhaled in his face, pursing her lips and eyeing him seductively. He bit his lip and she could see his chest rise with excitement as he inhaled. She moved away a bit and started looking around the room.

"It's a beautiful place."

"And you're beautiful too," Said replied, touching her arm.

Abdel-Jalil stood in the doorway carrying the bottles. He saw them next to one another and was immediately jealous. He looked at his friend, alarmed, and said to himself, "This whore wants to play schoolyard games with me? I'll show her who she's messing with." He faked a smile and put the bottles on the coffee table. He wanted to down a few beers so that he could loosen up and not be so reserved. Then he wanted to take his revenge by pouncing on Nezha right on the couch. He envisioned giving it to her rough and then throwing her out on the street without giving her so much as a single dirham. He'd finish with her and then head to the bus terminal.

As midnight approached, empty bottles were strewn about the table, the ashtray was crammed with cigarette butts, and two empty packs were crumpled on the floor. The room was cloudy with smoke. Nezha was sitting next to Said, and they were both drunk. Meanwhile, Abdel-Jalil was sitting across from them, even further gone: he had consumed twice what they had. Abdel-Jalil felt jealousy tearing him up as he watched them next to one another. What really irked him was how they were colluding to get rid of him. They were intent on ruining his night by waiting until he had to leave. He was not going to give in to their plan and leave them to have fun.

In his stupor he concluded that if he left after bringing over a girl for his friend, then that would make him a pimp.

Said looked over at Abdel-Jalil. "Did you forget that you have a bus to catch at midnight?" he said, slurring his speech.

Abdel-Jalil stretched out on the couch and looked at his watch. "I've missed it. I've wasted the cost of the ticket for nothing."

They became frustrated with his response and Nezha really wanted him to leave. She liked Said, and knew that the discoloration on his face made him feel inferior, and that drinking had given him the confidence to be with her. She remembered the envelope full of cash in the drawer in his bedroom. She moved closer to Said, obviously encouraging him to kick out Abdel-Jalil as soon as possible. To help move things along, she grabbed one of the empty packs of cigarettes crumpled on the ground, and tossed it back down.

"We don't have any cigs, and I need a smoke."

Said caught her drift. "Go buy us a pack of smokes," he said to Abdel-Jalil.

Bitterly, Abdel-Jalil guzzled the last of the beer in his glass and slammed it back onto the coffee table. "Where do you want me to buy cigs at this time?" he said, holding back his anger.

"There's someone at the top of the next street who sells them."

Abdel-Jalil hadn't expected his friend to turn on him like this for the sake of a prostitute. All those years of friendship suddenly seemed to go up in smoke. He felt like he was the target of ridicule, from a nasty whore and his ugly friend, who he used to feel sorry for. He felt his desire for sex transform into a desire for revenge, and he was going to get his revenge no matter what. When Said got up and wobbled toward the bathroom, he had the opportunity to confront Nezha. As soon as Said left the room, he directed a scornful look her way.

"I missed my bus because of you, so you're coming home with me," he said.

She ignored him and sipped her beer straight from the can.

"Who do you think you are?" said Abdel-Jalil, boiling with anger.

"What's it to you?" she said, stuttering from inebriation, her head swaying to and fro.

Abdel-Jalil didn't know what he was doing as he raised one of the empty bottles and approached her. "I'm going to break this over your head so you'll be able to speak clearly!" he yelled, losing control.

He raised the bottle in the air and would have brought it down on Nezha's skull if Said hadn't rushed back into the room, snatched the bottle, and shoved him away.

"Get away from her!" Said yelled.

Abdel-Jalil collapsed onto the couch, and then sat up and looked at his friend, shocked that he'd shoved him so roughly. He thought Said was rushing over to apologize and embrace him, but he stared him down, looking like he was ready to fight. Abdel-Jalil was utterly confused and didn't know what to do, so he remained on the couch.

"Why do you want to ruin the night?" demanded Said, circling the room. "Go and buy us cigarettes. Stop being an asshole."

Abdel-Jalil staggered as he rose. "Think carefully about what you're doing to me, Said," he said. "Are you kicking me out of your house for cigarettes, or for what? For this cheap whore?"

"Your sister is a whore, you fucker," Nezha replied immediately.

Before she realized what was happening, Abdel-Jalil assaulted her. He threw her onto the couch and was about to punch her in the face.

"Stay right there!" yelled Said, and he joined in the fray, trying to pull Abdel-Jalil off of Nezha, who was powerless to do anything except stare at the two friends and wait to see what would happen. They were standing face to face and panting loudly, ready to fight. Suddenly, Said unleashed a devious smile, opened up the CD player, and put on a CD of popular songs.

"If you don't want to go get us cigarettes, that's fine," said Said.

Said then grabbed Nezha, squeezed her, and they began dancing. He even started kissing her. Nezha responded enthusiastically, in order to infuriate Abdel-Jalil. Every once in a while they would both look at him, rubbing in how much fun they were having together.

Instead of leaving the apartment, Abdel-Jalil stayed in the kitchen, stewing over his friendship with Said. He was the only one who could get Said to open up, helping him get out of his isolation and instilling some confidence in him. Now Said was using this confidence against him! He was even trying to humiliate him—taking his girl, dancing with her, and kissing her right in front of him.

Abdel-Jalil heard Nezha laugh after the CD finished.

"Finally that jerk left," she said. "I hate jealous people."

Said hugged her, kissed her, and grabbed her ass. "Me too. We're the same, me and you. Forget about him."

He took her hand and they entered his bedroom. From his corner, Abdel-Jalil heard the sound of the bed shaking and creaking under their weight.

6

Bushra al-Rifiya grew up in the Rif Mountains among the fields of marijuana that produced Morocco's kif. As a girl, she loved school, and she excelled at mathematics to the point where she could help her father with the family's finances. However, once she reached puberty, she was forced to drop out to help around the house—or get married. Like other virtuous Rifian girls, her virginity was her primary worth. At eighteen, she agreed to marry Mohamed bin Bushuayb, even though she barely knew anything about him. It didn't even cross her mind to defy her father's commands. She never questioned marrying someone from their tribe, who, like her father, was involved in growing and selling hash.

Kif farming and hashish production were seen by the locals as simple agricultural work, like cultivating any other plant, despite the fact that it was illegal and farmers would be arrested if bribes hadn't been paid to the right governmental authorities. The farmers' lives changed dramatically once international drug lords realized how profitable the region could be, and they developed strategies to outsmart the authorities. They brought in small planes that would fly at low altitudes, under the radar of air-traffic control. Sometimes they would transport pieces of planes, one part at a time, for assembly on site, before a massive harvest was ready. When they weren't able to fly their product north to Europe, traffickers would drive a few hours along mountain roads down to the coast and load small amounts of hash onto speedboats that would shuttle their product to the nearest port in Spain. As the authorities caught on to these tactics they started improving their surveillance and outfitted customs agents with new gear and training. The drug lords countered with new schemes, using military-grade technologies and strategies. All the while, the price of hash on the global market soared and competitors swarmed, offering cheaper options from other countries—but the Rif Mountain region had secured its spot as the source of the best product in the world.

Mohamed bin Bushuayb was considered the perfect match for Bushra. He was handsome and mild-mannered and from a family known for their religiosity and simplicity that had deep roots in the mountains. Despite her initial aversion toward her husband, Bushra adapted to her new role as a wife. The real problem in their marriage became clear when, after three years, Bushra still had not gotten pregnant. In the Rif, a marriage wasn't considered genuine unless the wife became pregnant— and she should be on her second three years in. Bushra hated having to listen to advice about what she was supposed to do in bed in order to conceive, especially when her mother talked about the specific positions she had to try to enable her to conceive. And she absolutely refused to subject herself to the quackery of the local women. They wanted her to eat something called masakhin—a dish full of herbs, grasses, and strong spices—and just the strong smell made her nauseous.

A dispute between the two families took root, with Bushra maligned and shamed for being barren. She was comforted that her husband stood by her and apologized for his family's behavior. He promised her that one day she would get pregnant and become a mother. Bushra had no reason to doubt her husband's kindness toward her, until a lab analysis of his sperm confirmed that he was the one responsible for their inability to have children. She now understood why he had previously refused to accompany her to the doctor, fearing that it would be confirmed that he was the one to blame.

Bushra kept the results to herself. She didn't tell her husband that she knew the real cause of their problems. She didn't even tell her mother, who knew all of her secrets. Instead, she endured the hell that was the gossip about her rather than ruining her husband's reputation in his family and in their community. She knew that this could give her leverage if she ever asked him to leave Katama. He wasn't surprised when she eventually made this request. He had been thinking about a move as well. With all the issues the couple faced in the mountain community, their families didn't object when they announced their decision.

Her husband had been calculating this move for some time. Like generations before him, he started out as a simple farmer.

For years he only sold the hash from his plot of land and his uncle's plot. But recently, he had become motivated to do more with his life when he saw how some of the producers around him were profiting from the growing international interest in the Rif. He developed a new scheme: he'd buy the prospective harvests from other farmers in his community before the growing season even began, paying in full before anyone knew whether it would be a dry or rainy year. To start, he actually secured a loan from a bank. As the number of growers he acquired swelled, he gained the trust of a few international drug lords, and they in turn would pay him in advance. Through these deals he was able to secure his product and build up a stockpile.

Setting up this system led to his increased independence, and this was what allowed the couple to move to Spain, settling in Marbella. Here, he would no longer be Mohamed bin Bushuayb, the simple farmer. He changed his name to Mohamed "al-Sabliyuni." He became a savvy capitalist, selling at whatever price he wanted when surveillance increased and the demand for hash intensified. He was able to steer clear of suspicion because his business dealings more closely resembled those of a currency broker. He didn't leave a trail of incriminating evidence, even if the commodity he dealt in was green gold. He was able to secure his interests through a series of precautionary measures: he never met in person with his employees; he found a trusted representative in Katama who made advance purchases of the product; and he created a network of informants among the farmers who notified him when another farmer was going broke, being threatened with jail time, or simply falling on tough times. He would then offer the farmer a cash advance, as if he were offering a bank loan, even though it was completely biased in his favor.

Bushra didn't know anything about the business side of her husband's life. She didn't want to know anything, and turned her back on it. She was rewarded by a life of luxury, and her husband treated her extremely well. He complimented her incessantly, as if repaying her for her ability to bear life without children and never question his manhood.

They returned to Morocco abruptly, settling in Tangier on the heels of the Grand Campaign. It was at this point that Bushra started talking about adoption, thinking that this would make him happy. What Bushra didn't know at the time was that their return to Morocco wasn't just because of her husband's desire to return home, as he had told her.

The real reason was a briefcase that contained a total of three million dollars in different currencies. The briefcase was supposed to be exchanged as part of a deal that Spanish drug traffickers had made with Moroccan intermediaries. But the campaign had confiscated the entire hash yield and the intermediaries were all thrown in jail, so al-Sabliyuni thought that he'd keep the money without handing over the product, and then withdraw from the drug world and settle down in Tangier. He was hoping to live in peace since the drug traffickers were all behind bars. Since he had been in Spain, the campaign hadn't targeted him or put his name on the blacklist.

Bushra wasn't excited to be in Tangier, as it lacked the glamour and sophistication of Marbella. She was lonely and bored. She didn't have any friends and she dreaded the trip to see her family a few hours away. She knew that her husband was looking to settle down and spend less time on his work, so maybe now would be the time they could think about having a family.

When Bushra finally mustered the courage to talk with her husband about the possibility of adopting a child, she was stunned by his response. Instead of expressing his usual kindness and affection toward her, he told her he loved another woman and wanted a divorce. She couldn't believe the words coming out of his mouth. But what really shocked her wasn't his desire to divorce and marry someone else, but his insistence that he was not responsible for their inability to have children. This comment sent her into a rage. After all she had done to protect him, he was now claiming that he was virile and just had to find the right woman.

She didn't even try to challenge him. She knew that he was set on remarrying a lazy student named Maryam. She wasn't even pretty, but was just a thin Barbie doll, all makeup and cheap glitz. Bushra knew that if she stood in his way he might beat her or come after her. No matter what she said, it wouldn't matter. It was clear that she had made a mistake: she should have outed him back in the village in front of his family and the community, letting everyone know he wasn't a real man.

After the initial shock and fits of anger wore off she thought about what she should do. She decided her husband would get her revenge "served cold." So on that fateful day when he called her and begged her to not tell the police anything and give the briefcase to the guy coming for it, she decided to do the exact opposite. She hid the briefcase, filled with its millions, in a safe spot and headed to Detective Hanash's office.

Her husband had mentioned Detective Hanash's name quite often. What she knew was that he had led a massive, highly effective campaign against the drug cartels. The headlines in the papers featured the names of drug lords who were taken down, one after the other. Some of them fled the country; others were hiding out in the mountains. Their families were subject to all sorts of extortion and bargaining on their behalf—their wives' jewelry was stolen during the raids, along with anything else that was small and valuable. Rumors swirled of deals totaling hundreds of millions of dirhams, and payoffs being offered to senior government officials that included homes in Tarifa, Marbella, and other coastal Spanish towns.

Her husband never left the house during the most intensive periods of the campaign, when manhunts were plastered all over the news. He was glued to his cell phones, gathering information, recording the sums of money confiscated, the bribes being paid, and the promises made. "Don't worry," he would say to Bushra when he noticed her concern. "I know what's happening." But he never added any details about how all of this might affect them. He never gave her any directives about what to do if he were imprisoned, and she knew nothing about his assets. He was just like others in this business: he used crooked means to evade taxes and stashed his reserves in places that only he knew. Bushra had no idea how much wealth he had, although she was quite content with her luxurious lifestyle—the elegant clothes and expensive perfumes.

When she set out for Detective Hanash's office her intent was clear: pretend that she hadn't found the briefcase and was coming to the police about her husband's kidnapping. This would give the gang who kidnapped her husband all the incentive they needed to kill him. She'd then let the police in on the rest: that the man who called from her husband's phone ordered her to take the briefcase from its hiding place, and then she was supposed to call her husband's phone to receive her next instructions.

Before heading to the station, Bushra thought about her husband, and their life together. He hadn't treated her like his wife for a few months now. He could no longer stand to be with her, and was about to divorce her for another woman. She searched her soul for an ounce of sympathy for him, but found none. There was nothing left that bound them together—no love, no friendship, no companionship. What separated them was as clear as day: treachery, infidelity, mutual hatred, and lack of honest communication, not to mention his wanting a cheap divorce.

When the kidnappers called back, she told them that she had dug in the place her husband told her and hadn't found a briefcase. She was on the phone with them as she was driving to her family's house in Katama, with the briefcase next to her on the passenger's seat. They called back, and this time her husband was on the line.

"My life is in your hands, my love," he said, his voice shaking, weak from the torture the gang had subjected him to. "I won't leave you, I promise . . ."

"You were just about to leave me," she interrupted, feigning grief. "And now you say you won't leave me! I didn't find the briefcase. Try to remember better where it is. Maybe you left it at your new fiancée's place."

He knew she was ridiculing him. He went silent, as if he were taking his final breath.

"Say something." She mocked him further. "Did something bad happen to you?"

"I can't explain now. Please forgive me . . . If you help me now, I'll pay you back double, anything you ask. The sooner, the better . . . before they disfigure me, or kill me."

She could hear his scream echoing as if he were in a cavernous basement, and the call cut off suddenly. After a few minutes they called back, but she didn't answer.

After she hid the briefcase in a safe place in her hometown, her next step was to transform herself into a different woman before going to see Hanash. She first considered playing the role of a scared, forlorn woman—eyes teary and bloodshot, face pale, and trying to talk through her sobbing. This woman would wear any old jalabiya, cover her hair with a scarf, and rush to the detective crying, wailing, and screaming—"Help me, please! My husband was kidnapped!"—and she wouldn't be able to explain what had happened. This woman would only be able to add that an evil gang had hunted him, kidnapped him, and then asked for something she didn't have. But she thought that she would have difficulty keeping up this role of a grieving wife.

Once Bushra left his office, Hanash made a couple of phone calls and was able to verify that she was telling the truth about her husband's kidnapping and the gang who had taken him. Over the course of the following week the press devoted considerable space to what they called "the Sabliyuni affair." Detective Hanash enlisted all his informants and waged an all-out pursuit of al-Sabliyuni in Tangier and its environs. His men killed one gang member, injured several others severely, and imprisoned dozens who were connected peripherally. But Bushra's husband was killed by the gang members before Hanash could get his hands on him.

In the news of al-Sabliyuni's death, information indicating the presence of a briefcase that contained three million dollars never appeared and was completely erased from any official report. Even though this investigation was not as big as previous operations in which senior state officials were complicit, with the media being utilized as a mouthpiece to spread propaganda about how the government was "cleaning house," Hanash tried to make the Sabliyuni affair the investigation of the year. He leaked information to the press to exaggerate its scope, and used it as a pretext to ensnare other notorious bosses.

Bushra had thought that visiting Detective Hanash was going to be an exciting adventure. Yes, it meant taking some risks, but surely all would end well. But there was no turning back the clock, and a stifling sense of remorse overcame her as she considered the fact that she had been indirectly involved in a murder. When she decided to confess her role in hiding the briefcase to Hanash, he insisted that the true source of evil was the drug traffickers, gang leaders, and so-called 'businessmen' who were responsible for destroying families, poisoning the youth, and tarnishing the country's reputation. He explained that bringing these dangerous individuals to justice was a national duty that surely would be rewarded by God.

When future historians research the events of the Grand Campaign and carefully comb through all the news reports and other analyses, they will find all sorts of explanations and motives, but they won't find a single mention of Bushra and the briefcase.

Despite some ups and downs in the couple of years that followed, and despite Detective Hanash's transfer to Casablanca, Bushra's relationship with him blossomed and never lost its intensity. Whenever the detective got a chance, he would visit her in Tangier, and in turn she would visit Casablanca and stay at his secret apartment. When she visited, he would cut himself off from the outside world to be with her.

*

It was the second night in a row that Hanash had spent with Bushra in Casablanca (although his family thought he was in Fez), and he had barely slept more than a couple of hours. So when his phone rang and awoke him, it felt like an assault on his ears. He recognized the number and knew immediately that something serious had happened.

"Yes, sir," he answered with the utmost respect.

As soon as he finished the call, he put the phone down and turned to Bushra.

"That was the head of state security himself. He's requested that I lead the investigation of some heinous crime. . . . We'll continue this when I return."

Before she could answer, his phone started ringing again.

7

DETECTIVE HANASH HAD TO MAKE a quick transition from his night with Bushra to the challenges of getting to the crime scene—the traffic, the red lights, the impassable streets that were in need of repair. To make things worse, the crime scene was on a narrow downtown alley. There wasn't space for the police cars, ambulances, and forensics vehicles, let alone anything else. Hanash had to park his car some distance away and navigate through a dense crowd that filled the alley and surrounding streets.

A police officer noticed him and ran toward him, gesturing forcefully to the curious bystanders to clear a path. He stopped a couple of feet away and gave the detective a fervent salute, bringing his heels together with a click that drew everyone's attention.

"Sir!" he said, standing stiffly in salute, before leading him to the building.

The first thing that struck Hanash was how old the building was. It had damp, whitewashed walls. The windows looked out onto a dark alley that reeked of the acrid smell of urine, despite a sign that read "No Urinating" in coarse letters. He put his hand over his nose as he made his way inside. The alley was swarming with men, and as soon as they spotted Hanash, with his tall stature and bald head, they all straightened up and gave forceful salutes. They all knew that Hanash was a stickler for a proper salute. One of the officers rushed toward him and bowed his head in deference. He then led him toward the building's rickety wooden door.

"Isn't there any light?" asked Hanash loudly.

"No, sir. Should I get a flashlight?"

He received no answer. Once Hanash made it into the entryway leading to the stairs it became clear that his vision just needed to adjust. A bit of light snuck in from a side window.

The sounds of footsteps came from overhead, magnified by the wood flooring. When, with his usual confidence, he placed his foot on the first step to head upstairs, the sound made him fear that the whole building was going to fall on his head. He ascended gently, tiptoeing like a thief.

The apartment was teeming with so many officers that Hanash could hardly get in the door. The investigative team was hard at work, and the camera's flash was constant. The forensics unit, which had recently been reorganized, was moving around arrogantly as if they were some expert team from the show *CSI*. For a second he felt no one had noticed him, and wondered if his late arrival allowed the others to feel like they could run the investigation without him.

The first thing that annoyed Hanash was the draft. Upon arriving at a crime scene, he always closed the windows, so he wouldn't catch a cold. He stood in the doorframe as if he had the wrong address. He was astonished by the officers' silence, and almost yelled at the lead officer.

Inspector Hamid noticed him and, surprised, approached him like a lightning bolt, offering his apologies. He gave a firm salute to draw everyone else's attention to Detective Hanash.

"Good morning, sir," he said, bowing his head with the utmost respect. "You got here quickly."

Normally Hanash took three days off, minimum, when he was with his mistress and claimed to be traveling.

"I got back last night," he said, unconcerned. "What do we have, then?"

"A gruesome double murder. The victims are one female, one male. The male is named Said bin Ali, thirty years old, and the resident of this apartment. He worked in an electrical cable production factory in Ain Seba. The girl with him was Nezha al-Gharbi, twenty years old. According to the identity card we found in her pocket, she is a student, and lives in the Saada neighborhood."

"The murder weapon?" the detective asked, moving routinely to the next question.

"We haven't found it yet."

Before entering the bedroom to examine the two victims, he was struck by the sight of Officer Qazdabo, who was trembling in the corner. He went up to him and fixed his gaze on him. Qazdabo looked as though he might fall to the ground in discomfort. Hanash had prohibited him from saluting because, in his loose-fitting uniform and with his tiny stature, he looked like a comedian playing the part of a policeman.

"I . . . I'm sick, sir," he stammered, before Hanash could even ask. "I have a fever, a headache, and diarrhea, God help me!"

Hanash fought back a grin. Qazdabo looked like a cartoon character. He was nicknamed Qazdabo—an unkind reference to how short he was—and he always wore tattered uniforms that he bought secondhand. They were always extremely loose over his thin, short frame. He was in his forties and had been transferred to Casablanca from his native city of Taza as part of disciplinary measures. He took up residence temporarily in a vacated office on the top floor of the police station. For three years now he'd lived in this office because he couldn't afford to rent an apartment. He sent all his meager wages to his wife in Taza, who was raising their five children.

As he stood in front of the detective his hands were trembling and he was sweating in his thick wool coat, a completely unnecessary garment in this pleasant weather. This coat, in and of itself, was the source of a series of jokes at the precinct. Qazdabo looked off into the distance, not saying anything.

"I've told you numerous times not to wear that coat on the job," Hanash said, looking at him severely.

"Yes, sir . . . but I'm sick today. I was going to arrive late, but I thought it wouldn't be a good idea for both of us to be absent. If I'd known you were coming, I wouldn't have come. Sir, I'm really sick. I feel like everything is spinning. I'm barely keeping it together."

Under a different set of circumstances, Hanash would have found this funny. "You wore this clown jacket because you thought I wasn't going to be here?" he asked sharply. Without giving him time to answer, he turned to enter the bedroom where the murder had taken place.

"Detective, sir." Qazdabo stopped him pitifully. "Can I go? I have to visit the bathroom nearly every minute."

Detective Hanash glared at him, but his anger subsided a bit when he examined Qazdabo's woeful features, wilting eyelids, and fatigued posture.

"Get out of here," he said, pointing to the door.

Qazdabo turned to leave, put his hands in his huge jacket pockets, and rushed down the stairs, making a racket.

The moment Detective Hanash stepped into the bedroom a look of disgust spread across his face. What he saw surpassed anything he had expected. Blood was everywhere—on the bed, the walls, the clothes strewn about, and all over the floor. He realized some had even reached the ceiling. The two corpses were on the bed, one next to the other. The bodies had been naked, but a sheet had been placed over them. The detective withdrew the sheet and stepped back. Except for the suicide bombing scenes he had attended, where bodies and limbs were scattered everywhere, he had never seen such horror.

The male's abdomen was split open and his intestines were hanging out like those of a lamb on Eid al-Adha. Stab wounds covered every part of his body. It looked like he'd received a blow that had smashed his teeth and broken his nose. The female next to him had a perfectly intact face—she looked like she was asleep. But he couldn't bring himself to inspect her torso for more than a couple of seconds—her breasts were almost completely detached from her body, each clinging by a thin piece of skin—and he pulled the blood-soaked sheet back up toward her head. He stepped back, speechless.

As he looked again at the girl's face, he froze. It was familiar to him. The girl with the disfigured corpse on the bed was the girl from Hotel Scheherazade whom he'd caught with the bank manager—he was absolutely certain. He put the sheet back over her face as he tried to hide his reaction from the others. Even in death, her face retained the vigor of its youth. His senses went numb and his lips became dry.

He had to forget that he had previously met the victim, and make sure no one else knew. None of his men had been part of the raids this past Saturday night; that operation had been carried out by the morality police, who rarely worked in the investigative units. If the details of what had happened at the hotel came out—a senior police officer taking bribes—it would be a huge scandal that the press would run with for weeks. He knew he had to take control of this investigation with an iron fist, and he'd have to check all the details, big and small, himself, while allowing it to appear to proceed naturally without undue intervention. There must be no indication that he knew one of the victims, or that there was any link to the raid on Hotel Scheherazade. What happened there hadn't entered police records, and there was no way that bank guy was involved in this. He was certain the two incidents were not connected.

Detective Hanash understood why an eerie silence had settled over the room. In the face of such brutality, words seemed to lose their meaning. He shook his head in horror and left the bedroom. Hamid led him out, carving a path between the many officers milling about in confusion. He ordered a group of forensic specialists to stop working for a moment so that Hanash could cast his expert eye over the scene. The detective saw a coffee table with empty bottles on top, an ashtray overflowing with cigarette butts. He counted under his breath as he pointed at the bottles one by one.

"There was one other person, or more, with the two victims," he said, with absolute certainty. "No matter how long they were partying, this is far too much for two people."

"You're right, sir," said Hamid, nodding vigorously. "There are even more empty bottles in the kitchen, and some of the neighbors heard loud noises and music until one in the morning, or later."

Inspector Hamid was an obedient, opportunistic employee. He was very concerned with his appearance, from top to bottom. His hair was always perfectly combed back to Detective Hanash's satisfaction and he kept a permanently skeptical look on his face, all in an attempt to get himself noticed. He was in his forties and lived alone with his mother. He wouldn't even consider marriage until she passed away. Hamid was Hanash's right-hand man, and tried to memorize his every move as if there would be a test.

"Our men are out taking statements, apartment by apartment. There is another team interrogating neighbors from this alley and the surrounding area. And another is looking for the murder weapon."

Hanash wasn't interested in these mundane issues of procedure at this point. "The attorney general?" he interrupted. "Has he been notified?"

No sooner had he asked this question than he heard the sound of voices, footsteps, and greetings coming from the entryway and the stairwell. The atmosphere changed with the arrival of the attorney general and other officials, including the head medical examiner, who only came to the scene of the crime when it was extremely serious.

Detective Hanash hated it when the spotlight shifted off him and landed on a higher-ranked official in the room. Not to mention that he now had to kiss the attorney general's ass and fill him in on the details. He essentially repeated exactly what Hamid had told him. When the delegation of officials returned from the bedroom their faces were drawn, and everyone was in utter shock. They crowded around Hanash as though they were waiting for him to identify the killer, or killers, in one fell swoop. He didn't have a clue, but he had to propose something.

"Based on the configuration of this room, there's nothing indicating any sort of violent struggle. The furniture is in place and there are no broken bottles. Not a drop of beer or wine has been spilled on the rug. It seems that this is the room where the two victims, and someone else, maybe more than one other, hung out for a long stretch. This is clear from the number of bottles and ashtrays overflowing with cigarette butts. My preliminary assessment is that the murderer, or murderers, took the two victims by surprise as they were naked on the bed."

"There have to be fingerprints," said one of the officials.

"The forensics unit will find them," said another, with pride. "They have the latest tools and training to extract them."

"Right," the attorney general interjected. "The war on terror has forced us to modernize. Now we have the best forensics lab in all of Africa."

A heavy man holding a flashlight and wearing what resembled a space suit turned to them. It was clear to everyone that he was the head of the forensics unit.

"Since our lab was modernized we no longer have to seek outside help. Before that, we would have to wait more than a month to get DNA analysis confirmed from labs in Italy. Now we do these analyses locally, thank God. As you can see, the forensics experts are extremely meticulous. They find fingerprints, single hairs, and even traces of saliva. We now focus on details that were considered useless in the past, since we didn't have the tools to analyze them."

Hanash noticed that the officials—some of whom he didn't know—were whispering to one another about the horror of the crime as they shifted closer to the head of forensics. The detective wasn't about to lose center stage to this guy. He looked over the heads of the officials and caught a glimpse of one of his officers in the apartment's entryway.

"Zarouq!" Hanash shouted, regaining center stage. "Who is responsible for interrogating the neighbors next door?"

The officer moved toward the group, unfazed by the official presence, and delivered a half salute since the room was so packed.

"Sir, the apartment is empty," he said. "The residents moved out last month."

Detective Hanash nodded knowingly, even though he hadn't expected this response. He started scanning the room as if he were looking for something specific.

"Wherever alcohol and debauchery mingle, crime is just around the corner," he said, taking on the air of a philosopher.

He looked around and noticed Hamid feigning admiration, as if this were the first time he'd heard him say this.

"Who notified us about this crime?" Detective Hanash asked Hamid in a businesslike tone, signaling that the philosophizing was over.

"One of the building's residents who we have in custody, sir," Hamid said, standing straight as an arrow, his hands at his sides. "I did the initial interrogation, sir, and he said he lives on the top floor and discovered the crime scene when he was heading to work this morning. On his way down the stairs, he noticed that the victim's door was open, so he called out several times. When he got no response, he went inside and discovered the scene."

"Where is he now?"

"Bu'u is with him in his apartment upstairs."

There was considerable commotion when the head medical examiner exited the bedroom carrying his tattered leather bag. He was a short, stout man and was wearing a medical apron splattered with blood, like a butcher. He looked exhausted, and was clearly perturbed to find such a huge gathering outside the crime scene. He didn't know whom to address. He gestured toward Detective Hanash, indicating that he'd like to speak with him.

"What do you think, doctor?" Hanash asked, following him toward the door.

"A gruesome crime, no doubt about it," the medical examiner said, glancing back at the group. "You'll find all the details in my report."

"Could you at least tell me about the murder weapon and when it happened?"

"The crime was committed with a sharp object—a large knife, or maybe even a sword. The time of the murders was between midnight and three in the morning. The autopsy will verify everything with far greater precision."

The doctor didn't wait for further questions. He made his way down the staircase without even removing his bloodstained medical apron. After he departed, a group from the coroner's office entered the bedroom to place the corpses on gurneys and transport them to the morgue. It was a chaotic scene, and the arrival of the coroner and his aides added a few more bodies to the already packed apartment.

Detective Hanash felt a combination of exhaustion and bewilderment. He remembered that he had to call his wife. Work had frequently caused him to miss important family events. He'd known he wouldn't be present for the birth of his granddaughter, and now he probably wouldn't be able to attend the celebration they would organize in Marrakesh either.

He snapped out of his daze when the attorney general approached him, motioning that he wanted to speak to him alone.

"What are your thoughts on this bloodbath?" the attorney general asked.

The detective tried to clear his head and refocus on the crime at hand, which was still a mystery. His thoughts were scattered. It wasn't an option—as it had been with other crimes—to offer a confident hunch, because he feared subsequent developments would prove him wrong. There was also the fact that he knew the female victim. Keeping this fact concealed only intensified his caution.

"I think we have a crime of unprecedented brutality on our hands, the likes of which we haven't seen since the time of the Zweita serial murders, when the victims were horribly mutilated. The difference is that this is a double murder and the grisly way it was carried out might lead you to assume it was revenge. The evidence in front of us seems to indicate this, assuming that the perpetrators didn't cover their tracks and shift things around. If we just take into consideration the facts on the ground so far, it looks like a crime of passion whose motivation was jealousy or infidelity. This is my feeling, but we'll have to wait and see where the investigation leads us."

This was the answer the attorney general was hoping for, since Hanash was suggesting that it was an isolated incident. What everyone feared was that the crime might be tied to some larger criminal conspiracy. The attorney general relaxed and put his hands in his pockets, smiling at the detective.

"You are well aware of the smear campaign the media is waging against us these days. They're obsessed with how crime is out of control in Casablanca, and accuse the police of being negligent. But we both know it's just the opposite. Given this reality, I hope, detective, that you will redouble your efforts to solve this crime as soon as possible. We need an arrest to satisfy public opinion."

Hanash thought this was all a little premature. He and his men hadn't even concluded the initial neighborhood sweep, and the preliminary data hadn't yet been gathered.

"Each crime has its own particularities," Hanash said, avoiding going any further. "I'm going to give this case my full attention."

A satisfied look spread over the attorney general's face. He extended his hand and shook Detective Hanash's hand vigorously.

"May God help you. Let's be in touch about this case. As soon as you find out anything new, call me."

"Of course, sir."

The attorney general left with his entire entourage in tow. Hanash knew that most of those leaving could care less about this double murder. Even after the two corpses were extracted, the chaos in the apartment continued. The detective now resumed his role as the most senior official in the apartment, and felt a need to reassess the many threads of this case.

Hamid appeared in front of him, awaiting orders. "Should I close the window, sir?" he asked.

This was exactly what was bothering the detective—this light flow of air between the room's window and the open door. The detective sneezed and nodded. He took another lap around the apartment.

"Doesn't this building have a guard?" he asked.

"They don't have a full-time guard. There was a woman who came once a week to clean the stairwell, but she stopped coming a few months ago because the residents couldn't pay her."

"How many units are in this building?"

"Ten apartments, sir. According to one of the neighbors this building wasn't originally an apartment building, but a headquarters of some foreign company in the nineteenth century. It's more than a hundred years old."

This old building was pressed between two modern buildings on a dark and depressing alley. Its paint job was equally miserable. The apartments were small and dark, giving the impression of a haunted cellar. Hanash started up the stairwell with his right-hand man, Hamid. He couldn't believe how filthy the walls and floor were. There was a uniformed officer standing on the narrow landing of the top floor. When he saw Hanash he gave a firm salute that seemed to shake the building. The thud of his boots hitting the floor sounded like a gas tank exploding. For the first time ever, the officers saw a hint of fear in Hanash's eyes.

"What are you doing up here?" the detective reprimanded him. "Go downstairs and stand guard."

The apartment's door was open and its walls were a moldy green from the humidity. It was a single room partitioned into a living space and a bedroom by a cloth hanging from the ceiling.

The man who lived there was wearing a faded suit. His face was as white as a sheet and an unlit cigarette was twitching in his trembling fingers. Officer Bu'u was sitting in front of him. Bu'u had gotten this nickname, which meant the boogeyman, because of his terrifying face and his equally terrifying interrogation techniques, which made even the most hardened criminals confess. He had already thoroughly interrogated this man. As Hanash entered, Bu'u had his hand raised as though he were about to whack the guy.

Before Bu'u could salute, Hanash stopped him, ordering him to stay still, lest the whole building collapse.

Hanash refused to stay in the apartment for more than a minute due to the horrible stench of cat shit, which was intensified by the humidity.

"Take him to the precinct," he muttered to Bu'u, after taking a look at the fear-stricken man.

Detective Hanash headed toward the door and descended the stairs very carefully. He returned once again to the crime scene, where he spent another five minutes by himself inspecting every detail, looking for anything that had been missed. His mind drifted to a previous crime scene that had ended up being the first in a serial murder case. The murderer had wound up killing three people in an attempt to hide the initial murder. It wasn't unheard of for a suspect to commit a second or third murder to try to cover their tracks, especially if they feared being tortured by the likes of Officer Bu'u and others on the force. In the old days, most murders were the result of simple arguments or confrontations that got out of hand. It seemed that a major societal shift had occurred of late, perhaps a result of the Internet and the globalization of crime.

Detective Hanash lost his train of thought when his phone rang. He looked at the number and saw that it was home calling.

"Yes, hello?" he answered in a professional and resolute tone, indicating that he didn't have time to chat.

"Dad, you're now a grandfather! Atiqa gave birth to a baby girl!" his daughter Manar responded cheerfully.

"What!" he exclaimed, forgetting he was standing in the middle of a crime scene. "How is she? Did everything go well? And didn't they say she was having a boy?"

"Yeah, that's what her doctor said based on the ultrasound, but she had a girl. Everything went well, thank God. You can give her a call if you want. We all congratulated her and apologized for not being there, as the baby came early. We promised to visit soon."

"Your mother, is she feeling all right?"

"She's upset because she really wanted to be with her for the birth. Are you still in Fez?"

"I returned this morning, but had to go straight to work . . . one of the most horrific murders I've ever seen, and I'm up to my ears in it. Is your mother next to you?"

"No, she's crying in the bathroom. She feels really guilty about not being with Atiqa, even though there was nothing we could do."

"Stay with her. I'll call her later."

Hanash sighed as he hung up. How quickly and unapologetically time passes, he thought. It seemed like just yesterday his firstborn, Atiqa, had been a child herself, clinging to him, her eyes welling up when he tried to leave for work. Now she was a mother in her own right.

He looked over at Hamid, who had overheard the detective's call from home. He knew Hamid wouldn't say anything until he delivered the news himself.

"My daughter had a baby girl."

"Congratulations, sir!" Hamid hugged him, trying to give the impression that he was deeply moved by the news. Hamid then stepped back and saluted him so enthusiastically that he lost his balance. Hanash smiled reluctantly.

"She had a girl even though we were told it would be a boy," he said, still a bit stunned.

"God knows best, sir," Hamid replied.

"All right," said Hanash, shifting back to the crime scene. "Has anything gone missing here? Any chance the crime was motivated by theft?"

"I don't think so," said Hamid. "The doors had no visible signs of a break-in, and there is no indication that someone was rummaging around. The male victim who lived here, as you can see, didn't have much worth stealing."

There wasn't much left at the scene for Hanash to ponder. The real work was about to commence at the police station. He was confident his men were working feverishly in hopes of being the first to uncover a clue that could start unraveling this puzzle.

8

IT WASN'T EASY FOR DETECTIVE Hanash to navigate his way through the crowd back to car. He glanced at his watch and saw that it was noon. He was thinking about his daughter in Marrakesh in an effort to focus on the bright side of his new reality. He was elated that she was now a mother. Thinking about Atiqa made him think about his other daughter, Manar. When would she get married and have children? He had been giving a lot of thought to her situation in the past few months. And her situation was complicated by an ill-fated relationship with an irresponsible young man that had resulted in a broken engagement. This had not only tarnished her reputation; since then, she'd had no more marriage proposals.

Hanash sped out into the middle of the street, driving recklessly through the traffic. He tried to collect his thoughts and focus on the task at hand. After all, he was lead on this double murder. His competence and reputation as the head detective of Casablanca's criminal investigations unit were unquestioned, and he had a good success rate in solving cases. He knew that his excellent results were directly related to the years he had spent waging war against—and with—the drug lords in Tangier. He had climbed the ladder, occupying every rank in the force, until he took the lead on the Grand Campaign. This invaluable experience had taught him that all successful police work depended on three basic factors: a loyal second in command; a well-coordinated team; and an informant on the team whose job it was to report on what was going on behind the scenes with the investigative team.

He parked his car in his reserved spot at the central precinct. Even before he reached the main entrance, officers were preparing to salute, but he didn't look their way. He was thinking about Qazdabo, the missing piece to his template for a successful investigation. Qazdabo had always been the informant who eavesdropped on the other members of the team and reported back. He was the only one Hanash trusted to report on prospective leads or other secrets among them, because he was uniquely capable of casually extracting this information before it went public. His presence was even more crucial in this investigation, as Hanash needed to know about any chatter that might implicate him and his previous interaction with one of the victims. Qazdabo was the only one who could insulate him from a potential catastrophe.

Detective Hanash's spacious carpeted office was furnished with luxurious leather sofas and the walls were encased in wooden paneling. There was a massive bookcase stretching the length of one wall, holding a collection of beautiful books that gave the impression of being in a lawyer's office. Hanash had utilized his wide web of connections to furnish his office. It stood out in comparison to the others, which were unkempt and shoddily furnished. The other offices' walls were plastered with mug shots and other photos of dangerous criminals. They usually didn't even have a spare chair for a visitor to sit on.

Before sitting on his leather swivel chair, the detective carefully hung his jacket on the coat hanger and loosened his necktie a bit. He then leaned as far back as possible in the chair. He picked up the telephone and dialed his wife. She told him all the details of Atiqa's delivery, as relayed to her by their daughter. He then filled her in on his purported trip to Fez. He told her about receiving a call from the head of security himself, and how he had been totally absorbed in this horrible double murder since then. As had become customary in these situations, he then asked Naeema to guess what he bought her in Fez. But this time was different; she didn't entertain him and play her role in this worn-out game. Instead, she told him to save the gift for their daughter, and insisted that he call Atiqa to congratulate her immediately. She also prohibited him from expressing an opinion on the baby's sex, or asking about who had misread the ultrasound.

After he hung up, Hanash took a deep breath and removed from his desk a case file that was nearly finished. He yawned and stretched his limbs, readying himself to dive into the paperwork that had already come in about this case. Despite the gruesome nature of these murders, his preliminary observations didn't seem to reveal anything outside the usual circumstances in a murder case like this: there was alcohol, there was sex, and then there was murder. What was unique for him, as the image of the victims kept flashing through his mind, was the fact that he had met the female victim.

A sudden knock at the door interrupted his train of thought. He opened the door to find Hamid, carrying a bunch of files. Hanash asked him to sit down, and Hamid began detailing what they had discovered.

"The girl is Nezha al-Gharbi, a lady of the night, a prostitute. She has a few prior arrests."

"Has she ever been imprisoned?" asked Detective Hanash.

"No. The morality police arrested her once, but the prosecutor had the charges dropped."

"You have her address, right?"

"Area thirty-three, in Saada, the neighborhood known as Kandahar."

"Go there yourself," said Hanash. "Try to get a sense of the area and then bring in her mother, father, or any family members. And the other victim?"

"His full name is Said bin Ali. He was unmarried and worked at a factory that manufactures electrical cables in Ain Seba."

"There's only one factory for electrical cables and it's owned by a German company called C.E.B. What about his family?"

"We don't know anything yet about them except that they live in Madinat al-Qala. We're working with the police there, and they will inform the family. The male victim has no priors, and all of his neighbors report that he had an excellent reputation and seemed completely harmless. His landlord said that no one had ever complained about him."

"The girl who was murdered," Detective Hanash interrupted. "Was she his girlfriend? Had anyone in the neighborhood ever met her?"

"We described her to everyone we questioned but no one knew her."

"Why didn't you show them her picture from the digital camera?" Hanash interjected. "Her face was untouched. What's the point of this equipment if we aren't going to use it to speed things up?"

Hamid nodded and remained silent.

"Where is this neighbor who found the crime scene?" Hanash went on.

"He's still with Bu'u, who is taking a statement from him in an interrogation room."

Hanash got up and walked over to the window, gazing out at the busy street. It wasn't his style to show any sort of appreciation toward his men until the case was closed. In the early stages, he was always gruff and unsatisfied, and he'd never say what he was really thinking. With this case, it was even more important to hold his cards close, lest someone discover his connection to Nezha. His career, reputation, and future depended on this staying hidden. When it came to murder cases, absolutely no one would be spared.

Hamid looked at his papers, noticeably distressed that he didn't have more to report.

Hanash sat back in his chair. "Let's start with the families of the victims," he said, in a businesslike tone.

This statement marked the end of the meeting. Hamid stood up, gathered his files, and left the office.

After Hamid had left, Qazdabo appeared at the office door. His face was greenish and he wore a jalabiya, as if he were in the comfort of his own home.

"You plan on meeting with the detective looking like that?" said a security guard outside the office, as he looked him up and down, smiling.

"I'm ill," said Qazdabo, teeth chattering.

The guard couldn't hide his astonishment as he informed Hanash of who was there to see him.

Hanash paced around his office quietly, looking at Qazdabo in his outfit. He looked like a clown wearing pajamas.

"Are you out of your mind? Have you forgotten that you are a police officer in one of the country's largest departments? I have no idea why they transferred you here. They should have sent you to some desert outpost."

"Reprimand me however you please," said Qazdabo pitifully, "but I'm sick. I'm close to collapsing."

He wobbled as if he were suffering from dizzying nausea. Hanash gave him a chair and looked at him dubiously.

"I have a medical statement from my doctor prescribing three days' rest, and I'd like to spend the time with my family."

"At a time like this? When we need all the help we can get?"

Qazdabo trembled as he struggled to lift his head to even look at him. His pathetic state invoked amazement more than pity, and Hanash relented, recognizing how much his top informant was suffering.

"Fine. Leave the statement on the desk," he said, hoping to end this meeting quickly. "Go home, but when you return you'd better be ready to work."

Qazdabo lowered his head submissively and skittered out the door like a mouse returning to his hole.

After Qazdabo left, Hanash had a hard time putting his finger on what was frustrating him about this interaction. Even beyond his strange behavior and his alleged illness, Qazdabo seemed out of sorts. Could he have been aware of what went down at Hotel Scheherazade?

Directly facing Hanash's office was the office that Hamid shared with an officer nicknamed Baba. It was a small office that contained two workstations and an old-school typewriter from the previous century. There weren't any additional chairs for visitors. The walls were speckled with scribbles of black pen, and one of the curtain-less windows was partially shattered and covered over with cardboard.

Baba was an obese, dark-skinned man who had gray hair and beady eyes concealed behind thick glasses. He seemed content to stay at his current rank—after twenty years on the force the only promotion he had received was from officer to first officer. Despite this, he was full of himself, as if he were the highest-ranking policeman around.

"Get off your fat ass. Let's go," said Hamid, chiding him as usual.

"Where to?"

"To Kandahar."

"God help us," Baba replied, lifting himself out of the chair.

The neighbor who had first come upon the crime scene had been brought to Detective Hanash's office. He was standing in the center of the room as he hadn't been asked to take a seat. His face looked even more exhausted and anxious than when Hanash had seen him in his apartment.

"Speak! Let's go—out with it," Hanash said, as he stared him down suspiciously.

"All I can tell you, sir, is the same thing I've repeated to the officer and now the inspector," he responded quietly, clearly frightened. "The whole day is gone now, and I might lose my job."

Hanash always believed that anyone connected to a crime, however remotely, was guilty until proven innocent. "You're here to do what you're asked," he said. "Is there a problem if you have to repeat what you've already said? What are you afraid of?"

The man froze. He had heard some bad stories about those who lent a helping hand to the police, but he was hoping it wouldn't get to that point.

"This morning, I was headed to work as usual, and I was surprised to find Said's apartment door open a bit. I called out a few times, and no one answered. So I went inside and found that horrifying scene."

He started crying bitterly.

The detective didn't allow him any respite, and continued questioning him. "Your familial situation?"

The man seemed confused, and looked like he didn't understand.

"Are you married? Divorced?"

"I've been divorced for twenty years now. My eighteen-year-old son lives with his mother. She's remarried, and they live in Salé."

"What type of relationship did you have with the victim?"

"Just that we were neighbors and were respectful to one another."

"The murdered girl—did you know her?"

"Never seen her before."

"Did he usually have girls over?"

"Only God knows. All I know is that he was decent and polite, and everyone said the same thing about him."

"On the night of the murders, did you hear an argument or a fight break out, anything like that?"

"I heard the stereo playing music until about one in the morning."

"What songs did you hear?"

"I couldn't tell. The stereo wasn't on loud enough."

"What were you doing at that late hour?" The detective directed this question at the man like an accusation.

"I was getting ready for bed. I was almost asleep when the sound of the stereo woke me up."

"Had this happened before?"

"No, it had never happened before. Like I said, he was a decent and polite young man who didn't bother anyone."

"We think that the night of the murders someone else was with them, maybe more than one other person. You didn't see anyone?"

"No one, sir."

"Did he invite you to join them?"

Fear gripped the man. "God protect us from drunkenness and immorality. I am a pious, God-fearing man. I stay away from things forbidden by my faith."

Hanash was quiet for a moment, then continued: "What can you tell me about the rest of the residents in the building?"

"I don't really get involved in other people's business. It seems like the building is filled with respectable families."

"There's no one you're suspicious of?"

His horror at this question was written all over his face. "I have nothing to do with what happened," he said, exasperated. "I'm just a guy who lives in the building who had the horrible luck of stopping in front of the victim's door."

He nearly collapsed. He was physically and emotionally exhausted, and couldn't believe they hadn't asked him to sit down.

"You can go. But if you remember anything pertinent to the crime, anything new, call immediately."

The man nodded submissively and left the office quickly, as if he feared the detective would change his mind.

"Welcome to Kandahar!" said Baba as he struggled out of the tiny police car. Hamid shut his door and looked around. This neighborhood seemed more like a film set for a city hit by a tornado. When the local population saw the police car pull up, some people huddled around entryways and others peeked out from rooftops. The children stopped playing ball altogether. Baba zipped up his jacket and was already panting as he tried to catch up with Hamid.

They stopped in front of the house in question. The door was open, but a translucent drape hung over the entrance, through which they could see an old woman stretched out on a bed. Hamid knocked on the door and the woman feebly attempted to sit up.

"Wait, wait," they heard her say in a perplexed tone. Nezha's mother was clearly taken by surprise by the police officers.

"Does Nezha al-Gharbi live here?" Baba called in.

"Yes, sir, I'm her mother," she answered, nodding.

A group of nosy bystanders had gathered around the police.

"Scram!" shouted Baba. "Don't you have anything better to do with yourselves?"

A look of deep concern swept over Ruqiya's face, and she became impatient. "Who are you?" she asked, her voice trembling.

"The police," said Hamid, practically yelling, as if he were addressing someone hard of hearing. "Could we come inside and talk?"

"Please come in, gentlemen. It's good news, inshallah."

The two men hadn't expected the dwelling to be so run-down and miserable. It was so tiny that they couldn't move around once they'd made their way inside. "Worthy of its name," Hamid said to himself, thinking how these dwellings really did seem to resemble the burrows in Kandahar—small and dark, like a snake pit.

Baba, tired from simply carrying his own weight around, sat down. Ruqiya sat in front of him, also unable to stand on her own two feet. Hamid remained standing, disturbed by how dark the place was in the middle of the day. Nezha's mother leaned over to flip a switch and a yellowish light dimly lit the room.

"How long has it been since you've seen your daughter?" asked Baba, as he tried to find something to lean on.

"Last night," she said quickly, still hoping for comforting news. "Has something happened?"

"Did she tell you where she was going?" Hamid asked, leaning on the wall and staring at her.

She hesitated for a second, which roused their suspicion. They sensed that she knew exactly where her daughter was headed, and the kinds of things she got up to.

"What's happened to my daughter?" she asked, evading their question and starting to cry.

"Your daughter was murdered. She was found with a young man."

Ruqiya didn't scream or begin wailing. Instead, she lifted her head and hands upward in a strange motion and began loudly repeating a line from the Quran: *"God is enough for us; and how excellent a guardian is He!"* She repeated this more than ten times, as if it would undo what they just told her. When her throat ran dry she could no longer keep her composure, and started yelling in a deranged way: "My daughter! My daughter!"

The noise inside the house brought an even larger group of gawkers now. The timing coincided with the end of prayers, and a large group, including Ibrahim and his crew, filtered out from the mosque. They exchanged quizzical looks when they saw the people gathered around his entryway. Ibrahim rushed toward his house, shoving people aside to get to the door. His mother was still screaming when he arrived.

"My daughter is gone! She's gone!"

She kept repeating the same thing at an unbearable pitch filled with raw emotion. She fell into her son's embrace and the two of them nearly toppled over.

"What happened to my sister?" said Ibrahim, staring at the two men.

Baba realized he needed to stand, and he got to his feet, his huge belly protruding. "We're police officers," he said. "Your sister has been murdered."

The situation had gotten really claustrophobic with Ibrahim's arrival.

"Try to calm your mother down and follow us to the station," Hamid said.

Ibrahim couldn't control himself, and the tears started running down his cheeks.

"Who killed my sister? Who?" he asked, sobbing.

Hamid had already made his way outside.

"We don't know yet," Baba replied, noticing that Ruqiya had collapsed back on the bed. "Try to look after your mother and then meet us at the central police station as soon as possible."

When the two men exited, the nosy onlookers glared at them with hostility. The two kept moving, their faces expressionless until they sped off in the police car.

Baba looked at his watch and saw that it was one thirty.

"Are you hungry?" he asked Hamid, who was at the wheel.

As they left Kandahar behind, Hamid relaxed, even though the street was jam-packed.

"I can't stand driving in this city any more," Hamid said, lamenting the loss of respect for police vehicles in recent years. "You have to draw your gun now to get cars to make way."

"It's your hunger that's getting you worked up," replied Baba. "Where to eat, and what to eat?"

Hamid sighed and tried to pass a cab as he sounded the siren. When he got next to the cab driver he stuck his head out the window and unloaded all sorts of obscenities, then sped passed him, alarming bystanders.

"All right, what do you want to eat?" Hamid asked Baba.

"We're close to Restaurant Asmar. It's been a long time since I've had those kebabs."

"Give them a call," Hamid said.

Baba put in the order on his cell phone. Five minutes later they turned onto Yazid Street and parked right in front of the restaurant. It had the spit right out front, with smoke rising off it. An employee rushed toward their car carrying a plastic bag with the order. He leaned down and shook Hamid's hand vigorously, then handed him the bag. The officer thanked him with a nod. It was customary for restaurants to give officers free meals in exchange for added patrols in their area.

"Everything all right?" Hamid asked.

"Things are good, thank God. The patrols have been more frequent lately and we haven't seen nearly as many pick-pockets or beggars around here."

"God help us," Hamid said as he pressed on the accelerator. He opened up the bag and the mouthwatering smell filled the car.

"Security in return for lunch—this solution might please the government." Baba laughed, stuffing a kebab into his mouth.

9

WHEN RUQIYA AND IBRAHIM ARRIVED at Detective Hanash's office he pulled up a chair for her, since standing clearly wasn't an option. She settled herself down and sat completely motionless, unable to shift herself onto the backrest. She felt out of place in this well-appointed office. She clutched her son's hand as he stood beside her. Everyone in the room was dead silent, waiting for Hanash to finish a phone call.

He put the phone down and looked at Hamid, who was sitting opposite Ruqiya. He started flipping through the case files, which contained everything they knew up until now. He looked up at Ibrahim carefully and was surprised by how worn-out and disheveled the young man looked—his face was drained of color and his eyes were bloodshot.

"Are you her brother?" Hanash asked, monitoring him carefully.

Ibrahim shuddered, averted his eyes from the detective, and nodded, unable to speak.

"Do you have a job? Are you a student? What do you do?"

"I was a first-year English student, but I had to with-draw . . ." Ibrahim couldn't continue. He was about to break down.

"And what about now? Do you have a job?"

He shook his head in frustration.

Detective Hanash turned his attention to Ruqiya, who let out a groan before he even asked her anything.

"What did your daughter do?" he asked directly, as he stared straight at her.

Ibrahim lowered his head and his mother started sobbing.

"Answer the detective's question," Hamid instructed her.

She began nervously tapping the floor with her foot, noticeably conflicted. "What can I say, gentlemen?" she said, in a surprisingly unaffected tone. "Girls today are so difficult. Especially when their father is not around to do the disciplining, God rest his soul. She said she worked in a clothing factory." Then she started wailing again.

Hanash looked at Ibrahim, who was looking at the floor. He was silent, but his limbs were shaking, out of an intense anger. Hanash ordered him to have a seat next to his mother in hopes he'd calm down.

"Our goal is to find out who committed this crime. If you know anything that might help our investigation, it's better to tell us now."

Ibrahim's brow furrowed and his mother made a strange motion, which drew the attention of everyone in the room. It was obvious that she was having trouble getting something out.

"When was the last time you saw your daughter?" Hamid asked in a gentler tone.

"Last night," she said, turning toward Ibrahim.

"When did she leave?"

"Around five o'clock."

"Where did she go?" Detective Hanash asked, keenly awaiting her response.

"Since the day she stopped going to school I've had no idea who she hangs out with," she responded after a short silence. "I don't even want to make a guess and then be judged for it when I die."

"She used to hang out at a salon run by a woman named Salwa," Ibrahim said, not looking at anyone.

Ruqiya gave her son an anxious look, a plea not to implicate anyone else.

Hanash straightened up in his chair, his interest piqued.

"Sir, we don't want to accuse anyone of doing anything," Ruqiya said, looking straight at the detective.

Hanash ignored her.

"Were you at home when your sister left?" he asked Ibrahim.

"He wasn't home. I was alone with her," Ruqiya said, answering on Ibrahim's behalf.

"How was she?" Hamid asked. "Was she scared? In a rush? Did she receive any calls?"

"No, she was relaxed and her normal self," said Ruqiya, shaking her head.

Ibrahim knew that his mother was being careful to avoid any mention of what had happened the day before between him and Nezha.

Hamid repeated the other victim's name, Said bin Ali, twice, and looked back and forth between Ruqiya and Ibrahim. "Do either of you know who he is? Had you heard of him before? He's the other victim, and they were found murdered together."

Things took a turn for the worse. Ruqiya's eyes once again flooded with tears and Ibrahim buried his head in his arms.

"Oh God, how I struggled to raise her well," Ruqiya said, through her tears. "I wanted her to finish her education and live a respectable life . . . become a mother. But death shows no mercy. Her father was taken unexpectedly. He had an incurable condition and we spent every little bit we had on treatment. He was an honorable and decent man. In spite of our tough situation he provided the kids with everything they needed. I worked cleaning houses to help out. But after his death I developed kidney problems, and when things get bad it feels like nails are being hammered into my sides. And this poor boy had to leave university to take over his father's stall in the market, but they denied him his rightful place. Sirs, we struggle and barely get by and try to live an honorable life. My daughter was a good girl. Maybe she came under someone's bad influence."

"Are you talking about this woman Salwa?" Hamid asked, looking at his notes.

"I don't want to misjudge anyone, but she did go to that salon all the time to get her hair done."

The interrogation shifted to questions about Salwa. They wanted her full name, her address, and details about her relationship with Nezha.

Hanash stood up, sighed deeply, and put his hands in his pockets as he took up a pensive pose at the window, watching the traffic. This interrogation had soured his mood. It made him think about his daughter Manar, who ran a salon frequented by all sorts of young women. He completely rejected the notion that his daughter would be involved in the kinds of things that brought this profession a bad reputation. That said, he would have never given in to her desire to run a salon if she hadn't threatened him with moving abroad.

He turned around and looked at the miserable woman in her tattered abaya, who was still crying. He glanced at Ibrahim, and ordered them both to wait outside.

"Take them to your office for further interrogation," he said to Hamid. "I want a clear picture of the victim, her upbringing, and all the details of what she did the night in question. Call the mortuary and ask them when these two can see her body."

Hanash was sunk deep into his chair. He needed Qazdabo to bring him updates about what the team was up to, and what was going on behind the scenes. He straightened up when he heard a knock on the door. Bu'u had arrived with the first valuable lead. He saluted enthusiastically as he introduced the woman he'd brought in.

"This is Salwa, the hairdresser, friend of the victim."

Hanash recoiled at the word *hairdresser*, his daughter Manar's profession.

Salwa stood in front of Hanash in her black abaya with puffy eyes and her brow furrowed. She began to cry. Locks of bleached blonde hair slipped out from under the scarf covering her head.

"Do you have any priors?" Hanash asked, looking her up and down maliciously.

She blew her nose into a tissue without looking him in the eye and shook her head, still crying.

Inspector Hamid came in and unleashed on her. "Shut up! Enough with the tears. Stand up straight when you're in front of the detective," he scolded.

She started trembling. "I do have priors . . . but it wasn't my fault," she said, pressing her hands together as if praying that they be kind to her.

Hanash and Hamid smiled at one another. Just then, the phone rang. As the detective listened, he kept glancing back at Salwa.

"So. You were imprisoned for being a pimp," he said as soon as he got off the line.

"Oh God, sir, I was wrongly accused," she said, in a manner that infuriated the two men.

Hamid scolded her sharply and grabbed her arm violently, shutting her up. "You won't be leaving here in one piece!" he yelled, whacking her on top of the head. "When did you see Nezha?"

"I haven't seen her for days. We had a fight." She crumpled to the floor. She knew that Detective Hanash wasn't playing games.

"Take her to Officer Kinko in the basement," Hanash said, returning to his desk. "Tell him to hang her up until the morning." He looked at his watch. "It's time for us to go home."

Salwa shifted onto her knees, imagining a grimy basement with a floor saturated with piss, blood, and vomit, and she started talking.

"I did her hair yesterday," she said, still aching from the blow. "She told me that she had spent a terrible night at Hotel Scheherazade. She was with a customer who never paid her. She asked me to borrow some money, and I gave her fifty dirhams."

Salwa stopped speaking and tried to catch her breath as she adjusted the scarf to hide her hair.

Hanash froze for a second. This was the first time Hotel Scheherazade had been mentioned over the course of the investigation. He didn't want anyone to dig any deeper in this direction so he quickly changed the subject.

"What was Nezha's relationship with Said, the guy who was murdered with her?"

"God only knows. I've never heard her talk about this guy," she said firmly, hoping to sound convincing.

She cowered, putting her hands in front of her face, and shuffled farther back.

"Don't worry," Hanash said in a calm voice. "No one's going to hit you again. This would have been a whole lot easier if you'd talked to us from the start. Your friend was murdered, along with another man. Don't you want to know who killed them? Just tell us what you know and you'll be on your way."

Her face went pale and she felt a strange shiver shoot up her spine.

"Did she tell you where she was going before leaving the salon?" Hamid asked with a peculiar smile.

Salwa thought about everything she and Nezha had talked about yesterday, and she decided not to mention Nezha's problems with her brother.

"If you want to know everything about Nezha then go to La Falaise," she said. "Before leaving she told me about some problems she had with a bouncer named Farqash, who was demanding some sort of kickback from her. She was scared he was going to do something."

Baba was sitting in the passenger's seat of the police van as the team headed to La Falaise.

"This is the worst thing about this job," he said in frustration. "Who is going to compensate us for all this overtime?"

"You should call the minister of the interior," Bu'u chided him. "You want his number?"

Despite their weariness, they both smiled.

"I wish I was going to La Falaise to have a drink with a girl, instead of to arrest the damn bouncer," Bu'u said.

The van parked a couple of blocks away so as not to raise any suspicion. Bu'u, Baba, and two others headed straight to the front door of La Falaise.

It was around seven o'clock, which was when things got going at the bar. They weren't expecting resistance from Farqash, since he was well known and had an excellent relationship with the police. The owner of La Falaise was also in good standing with all the right people, and always paid his kickbacks on time. The bar, therefore, enjoyed special protection and the police over-looked all sorts of minor transgressions that took place inside. This was exactly what frightened the girls who worked there. They quickly came to understand that any dispute would not end well for them, given this special protection. And this was why Farqash remained calm, smoking a cigarette at the bar and flirting with Warda when the four men approached him. They encircled him in case he tried to make a move. The custom-ers sensed the tension and everyone froze. Suddenly, one of the scantily clad girls—cigarette in one hand, beer in the other—stumbled out of a corner toward the middle of the bar.

Looking right at Baba, she almost fell as she said, "Hey, you there, Romeo."

She had no idea that he was a policeman. A slap landed on her face and echoed through the entire place as she fell to the ground, the beer and cigarette flying into the air.

"Police!" shouted Baba. "No one move!"

Bu'u took out his handcuffs and waved them in front of Farqash. "Slowly, Farqash. Give me your hands."

Farqash stepped back until he ran up against the bar, and shot a quick look at Warda. "What do you all want from me? What did I do?" he growled.

In the blink of an eye Bu'u grabbed one hand and cuffed it, and the other men closed in on him until he succumbed. The customers saw that this was their chance to make a run for it, and rushed outside. This scramble made it clear how packed the place was, since it was hard to make out just how many eyes were following the action from the bar's dark recesses. The girls fled screaming, many of them barefoot and in skimpy outfits.

"Who's going to pay for all this?" said Warda, as she looked out at the overturned tables and the broken bottles on the floor.

"Just send us the bill," Bu'u said, laughing at her.

Back at the station, Hanash and Hamid grabbed Farqash from the two officers, keeping him handcuffed. Farqash's reputation preceded him, due to his long list of priors and belligerent nature. One time he even got off on a murder charge despite the huge amount of incriminating evidence corroborating his guilt. The rumor was that the owner of La Falaise paid close to ten million dirhams to get him off, since a guilty verdict would have meant the end of his bar.

Before either man managed to ask him a question, Farqash started talking.

"I know who sent you guys for me."

"Oh yeah, who?" ask Hanash, humoring him.

"The owner of Lafayette. He's always accusing me of stealing customers from his bar."

Hanash threw Farqash onto a chair, then leaned over and grabbed him by the handcuffs.

"This time you're going to be charged with two murders. Nezha al-Gharbi, who didn't pay up, and the guy she was with."

"Nezha was murdered?" he said, shocked.

Hamid paced around him. "Don't mess with us. Speak only when you're asked a question!"

Farqash gave his creepy smile, but a look of confusion spread over his face. "If it's that serious, then I'm all yours. Ask whatever you want. I'm ready to answer."

Hanash gestured to Hamid to start in.

"When did you see Nezha last?" Hamid asked.

"Last night."

"Where?"

"She came to La Falaise around seven or eight." Farqash fell silent, awaiting the next question.

"Go on," said Hamid tersely.

"I was waiting for her to give me the money she owed me, but she didn't."

"And why is she paying you?"

"I protect her from the druggies and glue fiends who would carve up her face. I pay off their boss to keep her safe."

"Keep going," Hanash said.

"I kicked her out of La Falaise when she didn't pay me."

"Where did she go after you kicked her out?"

"I don't know where she went."

"Did you see her again after that?"

Farqash remained silent for a moment, then shook his head.

"Where were you yesterday between midnight and three in the morning?"

"I didn't leave La Falaise until it closed around one. Then I went to Club Hufra in Ain Diab with Warda, the barmaid. We were there until six in the morning."

Hanash pressed a button and the door opened. A uniformed police officer entered.

"Take him to the basement," Hanash ordered.

Farqash slammed his boots on the ground in protest.

"Why are you keeping me, detective? Haven't I cooperated?"

The guard shoved him through the doorway.

"We'll let you go once we confirm everything you've told us," Hamid told him, as he disappeared down the hallway.

Ibrahim and his mother returned to Kandahar feeling like Nezha's ghost was trailing them. Their return happened to coincide with the end of evening prayers at the neighborhood mosque. The group filtering out of the mosque was mainly composed of Sufyan's young followers, hanging on his every word. They had been at the mosque since afternoon prayers, listening to Sufyan deliver one of his moving lectures on the eve of his departure for Syria. He spoke about how it was incumbent on any "real" Muslim to force their sisters, even before they reached puberty, to wear the veil and, even better, the niqab. He also emphasized that if you noticed a family member engage in any sort of immoral behavior or spout secular ideology, then it was your right to correct this behavior. He claimed that the severe drought that gripped the country was a result of the abominations of prostitution, homosexuality, and other corruptions endemic in society. He predicted that a massive earthquake or a catastrophic tsunami were on the horizon, and they would kill millions, destroying everything in their path. He charged his followers with recruiting more young people to follow the true Islam. At the end of the lecture he played a cassette in which an ISIS jihadi called his Muslim brothers and sisters to Syria and Iraq to purify the region.

Ruqiya wasn't even capable of opening her mouth to reply to the neighborhood women who greeted her. She couldn't actually make out whether they were offering condolences or insults. This crowd of people felt like an additional onslaught to her already shattered state. Ibrahim grabbed her by the sleeve and led her directly indoors, locking the door behind them.

As Sufyan passed Ibrahim's home he cast an angry look at the women gathered around their entryway. He could overhear one woman gossiping about Nezha's scandalous behavior. Sufyan berated her and then knocked on the door.

"Ibrahim, open up," he said.

Ruqiya opened the door and Sufyan immediately kissed her on the head, not giving her a chance to cry. He offered his condolences and sincere prayers for perseverance. He then turned to Ibrahim and embraced him warmly, as if congratulating him.

Sufyan grabbed Ibrahim by the hand and took him to the mosque. Once inside, he locked the door behind them. Sufyan again hugged Ibrahim and looked at him like he was a hero. Ibrahim was disgusted.

"What you did was incredible, Ibrahim!" Sufyan said.

Driss arrived at that moment, so Ibrahim didn't get a chance to reply. Driss boisterously embraced Ibrahim, just as Sufyan had done.

"She is now relieved of the dissolute life she lived, brother," Driss said.

"Remember your dead kindly," Sufyan scolded him. "All sin and dissolution comes from this unfaithful society."

Ibrahim tried to speak, but Sufyan gave him a cautionary look and pressed on his shoulders, preventing him from saying anything.

"After morning prayers tomorrow," Sufyan said, changing the subject, "I'm headed to Syria, inshallah. Let's spend this evening praying and reading the Quran."

10

NAEEMA WAS IN DESPERATE NEED of an attitude adjustment if she was going hide her true feelings—that her husband should be poisoned like a rat—when he returned home. She went up to the bedroom and began applying makeup in anticipation of his arrival, since faking her true feelings always required a new façade. She was not only angry that he hadn't been home in three full days, claiming he was in Fez, but she couldn't believe that he had gone straight back to work without even stopping at home to change his underwear. It felt to her that he'd finally given up caring about the minor details of this charade.

Her husband showed more interest in her cooking than in her. At this point in their marriage, he would sometimes show affection by sitting close to her and whispering disingenuous sweet nothings. And he made sure to compliment her in front of the children. After these minimal efforts he'd retire to his office, which had been converted into a separate bedroom. Naeema suppressed her feelings, as she had grown accustomed to trying to please everyone and would never cause a scene. She suspected him of infidelity and dishonesty, but liked being the wife of a powerful man. She found some solace in the looks of admiration and respect conferred on her by people in her social circles.

When Hanash entered the bedroom she was waiting for him in sheer nightwear that revealed her broad shoulders, large breasts, and taut thighs. He noticed that she had dyed her hair a reddish hue. He smiled as he approached her. She put her hands on her shoulders as if she felt cold.

"You have to let me and the kids go to Marrakesh tomorrow," she said. "It's shameful that Atiqa is there without family."

"Do whatever you think is best, Naeema," he said, his voice heavy. "I'm exhausted. I saw two disfigured corpses today. It was unlike anything I've ever seen."

She was silent, unable to process what he had just told her since her thoughts were elsewhere. He lay back on the bed fully clothed and pressed his temples. Under normal circumstances she would have fired off all sorts of questions about the crime and implored him to divulge every little detail. She sat next to him. He put his hand in his pocket and took out the necklace the female engineer from Hotel Scheherazade had bribed him with, and handed it to his wife.

"For you," he said.

He stretched out on the bed and closed his eyes so his vacant stare wouldn't give him away—he knew all too well that this was a pathetic attempt to express regret. She marveled at the necklace and then gave a wry smile, indicating she knew what he was up to. When he saw that her demeanor hadn't changed, he realized that things weren't progressing as usual. He took the necklace from her and hooked it around her neck.

"This cost a pretty penny and I've been waiting to see the gemstone glimmering on your neck." He dragged her over to the mirror. "Look how beautiful and elegant it is."

The valuable gift did nothing to purge her misery, as she was still intent on speaking to him about their daughter. She took off the necklace, inspected it closely, and held it in her palm as if measuring its weight.

"Where is the case and the receipt?" she asked, surprising him with a question he hadn't anticipated. "I'm going to give it to Atiqa and tell her it's from you."

He blushed. It would be impossible to convince her that he had bought it without a case or receipt, especially since it was such a valuable necklace.

"It's for you," he said intently, trying to avoid answering her question. "I'm going to bring Atiqa something else, myself, when I have time to visit."

To try to put an end to her questions, he drew close and tried to kiss her. She knew his tricks and shifted away, begrudgingly kissing him on the cheek.

Just then there was a knock on the door.

"Dad? Are you back?" they heard Manar ask.

Naeema rushed behind the open walk-in closet door and hid. Despite years of marriage she still got embarrassed if the kids saw her dressed like this.

"I got back a little while ago," he said, his voice maintaining its authoritative tone even in joyful times such as these. "Tell Tarek to get ready to go to Marrakesh tomorrow."

Naeema walked into the center of the room wearing a long dress.

"We'll leave tomorrow, really early, inshallah," she added.

Detective Hanash put on his pajamas. Naeema looked at him out of the corner of her eye.

"My poor daughter—if she hadn't delivered so early I'd be there now," she griped, wanting to remind him that he was now a grandfather.

"When you delivered Atiqa things went smoothly. No doubt it was the same for her," he said.

"Yeah, Atiqa's delivery sure was easy for you! You didn't give birth to her, and you weren't even there to know how painful it was."

He regretted bringing up this distant memory.

"I remember that I was on a case," he said, putting on his slippers. "God damn this job."

Hanash sighed heavily and reminded himself that despite life's ups and downs, he was blessed with a stable family. Naeema started picking up the clothes strewn about the bedroom as she pondered her past. She was the only one who really knew Detective Hanash. He had married her when she was twenty years old, after a very one-sided attraction. Growing up, he was the son of her family's neighbors, and he was the last person she thought she might marry. To this day she remembered how mean he was as a kid. She only succumbed to the marriage after all the pressure her family put on her.

Detective Hanash woke up before everyone else the next morning. He went down to the garden to play with Karet, his beloved and spoiled German shepherd. Karet had been a police dog, and was extremely well trained and obedient. He was alert at all times and had a distrustful stare.

The detective looked up toward the kitchen, a room somewhat detached from the rest of the house.

"Wafa!" he called to their maid. "Where are you?"

Wafa rushed out and stood in front of him. She was in her twenties and from a Bedouin background. Her face was sallow and her eyes were slightly bloodshot, as if she'd been crying.

"Yes sir," she mumbled.

She always assumed the same posture in his presence—she'd stand submissively with her eyes fixed on the ground in front of her. She didn't behave this way because she was treated harshly, but this timid attitude was a result of the difficult life she'd had. Her father had murdered her mother following some trivial argument. He was now in prison, serving a thirty-year sentence, and her mother was resting peacefully six feet underground. Hanash had intervened on Wafa's behalf after she spent three nights sleeping in the precinct with nowhere to go. He had felt sorry for her, and after consulting with his wife, brought her back to work in their home. Naeema promised her she'd have a place with them until she could find her a suitable husband.

"After the family leaves for Marrakesh," Hanash told her, "let Karet off his leash in the garden and give him his food as usual. Do not open the door for anyone."

"Yes, sir."

"Did you wash the car windows?"

"Yes, sir."

He gave a nod, indicating his satisfaction. Wafa headed back into the kitchen and Manar came outside wearing jeans and a revealing tank top, as was the fashion these days. He avoided looking in her direction, which she knew meant he didn't approve of her clothes.

Manar was an extremely skinny twenty-seven-year-old. She had a light olive complexion, taking after her father, and brown eyes. Her hair was always perfectly done, which was a professional obligation. She hadn't finished high school due to her infatuation with this wealthy brat of a kid who Hanash had found no way of getting kicked out of the country, despite his best efforts. Unable to sway her the least bit, he and Manar arrived at an agreement in which they would get engaged. But Manar's engagement to the man of her dreams eventually extended beyond the two-year mark, and it became clear, even to her, that this guy was an irresponsible idiot who took advantage of women. The engagement was broken off quietly. Hanash didn't speak to his daughter for an entire month after this episode. When she started talking about leaving the country he got nervous, and came to a compromise with her. He told her to choose a profession to keep her busy and he'd support her. She chose hairdressing, a choice he reluctantly accepted, since it did not have the greatest reputation.

The family piled into the car to head to Marrakesh, and Tarek got behind the wheel.

"Don't forget, it's my car," Hanash warned him. "Drive carefully and don't get angry if someone cuts past you."

"Let's go!" said Naeema impatiently.

She was sitting in the back, while Manar was in the passenger's seat next to her brother. Naeema wanted to get on the road, fearing that any little thing might delay their departure, as had happened plenty of times before.

As the noxious smell entered his nose Hanash hastily closed the police car's windows. Just up ahead he saw an oddly colored cloud that had enveloped the industrial area of Ain Seba, just outside Casablanca. This area was considered the most polluted place in the country. He drove on until he found a spot to park the car in front of the electric cable factory.

He could have sent one of his men to the factory but with this investigation he really wanted to be on top of any new leads.

The factory's director welcomed him into his large office. He was a handsome young man wearing a crisp white shirt and a red tie. Hanash introduced himself and looked straight into the director's eyes, in a disarming manner.

"Do you have an employee by the name of Said bin Ali?" he asked.

The director repeated the name to himself a couple of times. "Yes, he works here." He then informed him that Said was off that day, and would resume work the next morning.

"Well, he won't be working today or tomorrow. He was murdered yesterday."

The director froze in his chair, frightened that he might be accused of something. Hanash was pressed for time, so he quickly summarized the details of the murder for him.

"He was a serious guy who valued his job," the director reflected.

"Did he have any enemies here at work?" Hanash asked, transitioning to the real purpose behind his visit.

"None," the director said confidently. "On the contrary, the employees in this factory are like one big family. We are keen on maintaining good relationships between all employees since this is crucial to team morale. Even though this factory is in Morocco, it's run with a German mindset. I studied management in Germany and was trained to implement it."

Hanash gave him a smile of admiration. "I don't need to interrogate every employee," he said, "but the victim must have had some close friends with whom he worked."

The director pressed a button, which opened a door, and a security guard came in. His face was drawn, and Hanash saw that he'd heard everything from behind the door.

"The detective has just informed me that Said bin Ali was murdered yesterday in his home," said the director, his voice heavy with sadness.

The security guard slumped slowly into a chair.

"I want to know everything about Said," Hanash stated, in a businesslike tone.

The guard was distraught by the news and had trouble getting his words out. He praised Said's work ethic as he fought back tears.

"Tell me the names of his friends here at the factory," Hanash interrupted unsympathetically.

"He had one very close friend. They were always together."

"What's his name?"

"Abdel-Jalil Kazar," the guard said, his voice trembling.

"Bring him in immediately," said Hanash.

The guard hesitated, intimidated by the detective's severe tone.

"He's also off today," the director intervened. "He isn't scheduled in until eight tomorrow morning."

Hanash had intended to ask more questions, but suddenly changed his mind. He took out his notepad and asked for Abdel-Jalil's address and phone number, jotting them down quickly.

"If anything comes to mind that could be related to this investigation, call the central precinct immediately."

It was two in the afternoon when he got back to his car, and he felt his stomach rumbling from hunger. He sat facing the steering wheel for a moment, trying to organize his thoughts about the case before deciding where to have lunch. On normal days, even when it was nonstop, he would sometimes give in to his wife's insistence that he eat with the family at home. After lunch, he'd stay at the office into the evening, even though four thirty was the official end of the workday. He usually didn't leave until after six.

Before starting the engine to leave the industrial area he called the precinct and asked for a junior member of his team, Officer Miqla.

"He had a close friend named Abdel-Jalil Kazar," Hanash said. "I want him at the precinct before I get back."

"Yes, sir. You'll find him waiting."

As Hanash drove out of Ain Seba the grayish-yellow haze of pollution gave way to a clear blue sky and the sun's bright rays. "The only clouds in the sky are toxic manmade clouds," he said to himself. As he thought about the atmosphere, he remembered that not a single drop of rain had touched the ground this November, and the month was nearly over. If the drought continued like this, he'd never have another summer vacation. Water shortages caused massive migration into Casablanca from the surrounding villages. The unemployment crisis would intensify, and crime would increase.

He headed toward the posh beachfront neighborhood of Ain Diab, with its wide avenues lined with hotels and nightclubs. He left his patrol car in a no-parking zone. Life in Casablanca had gotten worse by the day, but its residents clung to it, and still considered it the country's most beautiful city. He had to confess that he didn't love the city, even though it was his hometown. He preferred Tangier.

He set out on foot toward a narrow side street filled with many of the city's best restaurants. He walked briskly, as if he were on a case. He popped his head into Restaurant Shati to look around, and realized he'd need to make other plans—the place was completely packed. But the owner of the restaurant, a man nicknamed Rubio, spotted Hanash and pulled him inside without saying a word. He led him through a hallway to his office. Rubio got his nickname because his light skin and blue eyes made him look like a Viking. After he'd closed the door behind him, he hugged Hanash warmly.

"You were going to walk straight back out? How could you?" Rubio exclaimed in his Tangier accent. "You're more important than all those customers out there combined. Had I known you were coming, I would have prepped your favorite table."

"To be honest," said Hanash, "I don't really have an appetite. I was passing by and I thought I'd pop my head in to say hello."

"You think I'm going to let you leave with an empty stomach? An order of seafood is already on the way."

Rubio nimbly cleared the desk and excused himself to oversee the preparation of the food personally.

Hanash looked around the small office. It had a warmness and intimacy to it. He relaxed on the leather office chair, and suddenly it felt strange to be sitting here in this office, in the middle of a double murder investigation. He knew his men were working like dogs, but no one had called him, so there was nothing new that required him to return to the station immediately.

An employee entered the office, mumbled a greeting, and began transforming the desk into a dining table. Hanash was so wrapped up in his thoughts that he didn't even notice when a waiter entered to place a delicious meal in front of him.

Every time Hanash came to this restaurant he was reminded of the golden age in Tangier when he had headed the drug-trafficking team. He sat there with this amazing seafood in front of him, but had no appetite. He hadn't even removed his jacket; he'd only slackened his necktie a bit. He thought about his friendship with Rubio. He enjoyed Hanash's full protection, since the days when this deeply devout Djibili man was a big-time hash dealer in Tangier. Rubio had done it the smart way: he carried out a few big jobs from which he made millions and then, based on advice from Hanash, he got out of the game for good right before the Grand Campaign. Rubio then moved to the country's economic capital, Casablanca, where he laundered his money. He now owned a premier hotel, two gorgeous cafés, real estate, and this modern restaurant. Rubio may have successfully purged himself of certain characteristics of his country-bumpkin upbringing, but he still couldn't get rid of his mountain accent, and his friends in Casablanca let him know it. He and Hanash had a strong bond. Rubio was the only one who really knew Hanash's past, and Hanash was the only one who really knew Rubio's.

"You're not eating," said Rubio as he entered, closing the door and sitting on the small chair facing the detective.

"I know the food is delicious, but I don't have an appetite," Hanash replied, sighing.

"You're not yourself. What's up? You know you can tell me anything. Are you having trouble at work?"

The detective stared at Rubio and smiled.

"I'm now a grandfather," he said. "My daughter gave birth to a little girl. Naeema and the kids are with her in Marrakesh."

"Congratulations, brother!" Rubio embraced him and kissed him on the cheeks in celebration.

"I was going to go with them, but a nasty double murder got in the way."

"You should have shut off your cell phone and gone to see your daughter."

Officer Miqla returned empty-handed from Abdel-Jalil's apartment. He left a summons letter, but that was all he could do. Every attempt at reaching Abdel-Jalil by phone resulted in the same automated message: "The number you dialed is out of range. Please call later." His inquiries with the neighbors didn't turn up anything of note.

"Has this guy vanished?" he thought to himself, annoyed. He wondered if Abdel-Jalil had gotten to the neighbors already, convincing them not to say anything.

Miqla knew that Abdel-Jalil had the day off, so it was possible he'd left the city. He left the summons requesting him to present himself at the precinct at eight the following morning, and phoned Hanash to update him.

"He's the male victim's closest friend," he barked at Miqla angrily. "He's the key to solving this."

"If you want, we can put eyes on the place overnight."

"We'll follow up tomorrow. If he doesn't show up in the morning, he'll be our primary suspect."

Hanash arrived home around ten o'clock. Karet greeted him with a loud bark, letting him know that he was late for their evening walk. Before heading inside he inspected every dark corner of the villa's dimly lit garden. This was a habit he had developed in Tangier when he was involved with various drug traffickers. He used to receive at least one death threat per month. Despite the years that had passed since his transfer to Casablanca, he was still worried about payback.

In Tangier he always knew exactly who was threatening him. He would summon them to the office and turn the tables by threatening them himself. This was all part of the psychological warfare involved in the drug game. The traffickers would try to intimidate Hanash to reduce the kickbacks they paid, and to prevent him from siding with one group over another. After all, drug trafficking was not just about exporting your goods across the Mediterranean, it also came down to building local influence. Whenever the hash supply decreased, the price skyrocketed due to increased demand. These shifts in the market were often carefully orchestrated by Hanash and the organizations that paid the highest kickbacks.

As he petted Karet and played with him, he wondered why each murder investigation rattled him so deeply. He always felt like every corpse he encountered on the job might include some hidden message, indicative of his own death. As he went through the motions on each investigation, regardless of its circumstances, he was plagued by the idea that there might be some thread leading back to the drug traffickers in Tangier.

The flip side was that this perpetual fear of retribution burning him up inside could only be subdued by solving the murder. This was the real secret to his dedication and success, as each murder felt like a personal attack. But with this case, he did have a real connection to the female victim, and was trying to keep it out of the case files. If this was discovered, the scandal would be catastrophic, and his professional life would be over.

Hanash was more than just a cautious and careful man. His suspicion verged on paranoia. He couldn't live without informants, even in his own home. His top domestic spy was his maid, Wafa, and he took her aside every evening when he returned home to hear her report about what his wife and kids had done when he was at work. He never skipped a report, no matter how trivial—it was the final piece of his workday.

Wafa appeared and asked him if he'd like her to prepare his dinner.

"What did you cook?"

"Mrs. Naeema called me from Marrakesh and told me to make you a kofta and egg tagine."

This sentence struck a strange chord. Despite being far away in Marrakesh, his wife had not only thought about his dinner, but had called to tell Wafa what to cook him. As if he were a baby in need of feeding.

He stretched out on the bed in his work clothes and his mind drifted. He had lived most of his life without looking back, and rarely was he alone or felt lonely. Being alone gnawed at his nerves because he would think about his life and start reevaluating everything he'd done and everyone around him. He had trouble looking at the world from any other perspective than as a detective. He started thinking about Salwa—the bleached-blonde hairdresser who used her salon as a recruiting center for prostitution. He thought again about his daughter Manar, the hairdresser. He recalled how he had advised her to think about opening a hairdressing school, so at least she could teach and not just run a salon. She had to get married soon, he thought to himself—a suitable man was bound to come along soon. It pained him to think about her broken engagement. She had left her studies without getting a degree because of this stupid relationship. "Was she even still a virgin?" he wondered.

Hanash got up and headed out on his evening walk with Karet. The streets of Casablanca were nearly empty at this time of night, save for some inebriated drivers flying through the streets. He cut across Zarqatouni Street, one of the city's main arteries, and passed by his central precinct. He wasn't alarmed to see light coming from his office window, since he knew that the cleaning crew must be working. At the end of the street he turned onto a side street and let the dog off the leash. He wasn't really aware of where he was going until he found himself in front of his daughter's salon. No doubt she entrusted an employee with running the place while she was away. It was a beautiful place occupying a ground-floor store-front on March 2nd Avenue. There were neon lights blinking from behind the glass, even though the salon was closed. He had never been so generous as when he had financed this salon. He hired what seemed like thousands of people to ren-ovate and equip the place. His generosity wasn't only to satisfy his daughter, however: he'd used the salon to launder some of the small fortune he'd acquired in Tangier.

He stood in front of the salon, Karet panting by his side, and thought about everything that had happened recently. He thought about his firstborn, Atiqa. Raising her had been so much easier than Manar, but this was probably because Atiqa had married and left the house before Hanash's newly accu-mulated wealth could influence her behavior, as it would her siblings. Atiqa grew up as they were struggling to make ends meet. She was born when he was just an officer. They were living in a dank apartment in a lower-class neighborhood, and he wasn't able to pay the monthly bills without the mea-ger kickbacks he got from low-end drug dealers and hustlers.

These kickbacks were equivalent to tips a waiter in a café might receive. Maybe that's why Atiqa became so obedient, like her mother. As he let himself wander down memory lane he found himself taking out his key to the salon. He had never told Manar that he had one made. He looked left and right, like a thief, and left Karet at the entrance to stand watch. A mixture of women's perfumes and scented cleaning products assailed him as he entered. When he turned on the lights, he found himself next to a coatrack on which hung a bunch of white aprons used for hairstyling.

The elegance of the salon really surprised him—it had plush leather chairs, massive mirrors, and television screens scattered around. One of the screens had been left on, and it was playing an instructional hairstyling video. He watched a couple of scenes, as a male hairstylist combed, and then trimmed, a beautiful woman's hair. He hesitated for just a second before making his way to his daughter's desk, which was separated from the hairstyling area by a glass divider, allowing her to keep an eye on the entire place. He felt like a thief searching for something valuable, so he sat down on his daughter's leather swivel chair and began rocking back and forth thinking about what do to. He didn't have a good idea why he was there in the first place. His mind was scattered and he felt strange about intruding into Manar's personal work space. He opened the top drawer of her desk and took a peek at the contents. He stiffened when he saw a photo of a handsome man. This was exactly what he had feared: finding something that would enrage him. He slammed the drawer closed. This wasn't what he was looking for, but now his anger was stoked. He imagined his daughter embracing this guy right there in a salon financed by bricks of hash!

How many dark nights had passed, how many threats, and how many risks he had taken with his own life and his family's future.

11

DETECTIVE HANASH ARRIVED AT HIS office at eight in the morning. None of his men had called the previous night, meaning there were no new developments.

He found all the daily newspapers on his desk. He started scanning the headlines and saw that every single paper had the crime on its front page, with contradictory details, as usual. What perturbed Hanash was that that one paper had printed a photo of the two victims, and gave details about the crime that could have only come from someone closely connected to the investigation. Who had leaked this information to the paper, and for what price? What pissed him off even more was that someone had taken his quote—"Wherever alcohol and debauchery mingle, crime is just around the corner"—without attributing it to him.

He pushed the papers aside and opened the case file in front of him. Except for some interrogation notes and photographs of the victims, it contained nothing new. There was still no mention of what had happened at Hotel Scheherazade. Today, he thought, had to be the decisive day in this investigation. A lot was riding on the testimony of the male victim's friend, and if he didn't show up, suspicion of guilt would fall squarely on him.

Hanash was in no hurry to summon his men for nine o'clock. He knew that they had worked several hours of over-time, and they weren't even on the clock for these extra hours. No doubt Hamid had sent men to investigate Farqash's alibi concerning where he was during the time of the murders.

At five past nine Hamid opened the door and gave a determined salute.

"Good morning, detective."

Hanash returned the salute and motioned for him to sit down. He enjoyed the fact that Hamid dressed sharply, in an effort to imitate him. The main difference between their wardrobes was that the detective's suits were all by famous designers, whereas Hamid wore the most fashionable imitation versions he could find.

"What's the latest?" asked Hanash, moving the case file aside.

"What's new is that Farqash's alibi came back clean, one hundred percent," he replied, rubbing his hands together. "I sent Bu'u and Miqla to Club Hufra, and several witnesses confirmed that he got there around one in the morning with Warda, the bartender from La Falaise."

Annoyed, Detective Hanash slapped the back of his chair.

"We haven't gotten the medical examiner's report to ver-ify the time of death," Hamid said regretfully, "but Warda confirmed that Farqash didn't leave La Falaise all evening, not for a single moment. Then they left together for Ain Diab in a taxi. A doorman who worked on the same street as La Falaise corroborated everything. He said he saw Farqash and Warda hailing a cab around one o'clock."

"Keep him in temporary detainment anyway," said Hanash firmly. "Don't let him out until the twenty-four hours is up. Just in case we need him."

Hamid also informed Hanash that the male victim's father had arrived from Madinat al-Qala. Hanash dispatched Bu'u to take him to identify the body before bringing him in for questioning.

There was a knock at Hanash's office door, and he opened it to find a security guard saluting him.

"A person with a summons is here, sir," he announced, as if he were reading a news report. "He says his name is Abdel-Jalil Kazar."

"Bring him straight in," Hanash replied.

When Abdel-Jalil entered the office, the first thing that struck both Hanash and Hamid were his teary eyes, meaning he knew what had happened. They looked at him closely. He was a clean-cut man in his thirties, and was quite handsome. Hamid requested his national identity card and the summons. Hanash didn't take his eyes off Abdel-Jalil, readying himself for an interrogation.

"All right," said Hanash. "You're crying, so you know what happened."

Abdel-Jalil nodded.

"Who told you?" asked Hamid.

"I called the factory to tell them I'd be late coming in because of the summons, and the director told me what had happened to Said."

He could no longer suppress his emotions and burst into tears. Hamid placed the identity card and summons on the desk and exchanged a look with Hanash.

"Where were you yesterday?" the officer asked, in an accusatory tone.

"I was visiting my family in Fez. I just returned this morning."

"When was the last time you saw your friend?" asked Hanash.

"Sunday evening . . ." Abdel-Jalil's voice trailed off, and he took a moment to compose himself. "Could I sit down?" he asked.

They didn't answer.

"You were saying?" Hamid said gruffly. "The last time you saw your friend was Sunday night . . . and?"

"After we finished work we went to go eat at Baaroub's, like we always do when we get our wages at the end of the month. We ate together, and then around eight we went our separate ways." He started choking up again. "If I knew what was going to happen, I wouldn't have left him."

Hanash interjected: "The girl who was murdered with him, Nezha al-Gharbi—did you know her?"

"I didn't know her," he said, shaking his head and wiping away his tears.

Hanash opened up the case file and took out a photo of Nezha. He passed it to Hamid, who then showed it to Abdel-Jalil. They watched him closely as he looked at the photo. He shook his head, verifying he didn't know her.

"Said was more than a brother to me," he said, holding back tears. "Who could have done this?"

"After you parted ways, where did you go?" Hanash asked.

"I went to the bus terminal and got a ticket for the midnight bus to Fez."

"And you went to Fez?" asked Hanash.

"Of course I went to Fez. I nearly always go on the first of the month, after I get my wages, to visit my family and give them what I can to help out. I was going to go on Saturday night, but our weekly day off was postponed until Monday because of all these last-minute orders."

"So, you traveled to Fez at midnight and then you were with your family?" Hamid asked.

Hanash and Hamid exchanged a curious look.

"What's your family's address in Fez?" Hamid demanded.

Abdel-Jalil dictated the address and Hamid scribbled it down in his notebook. Hanash got up, opened the curtains, and stared out into the busy streets. He needed a few moments to think. This young man had thrown him for a loop, as he seemed to be telling the truth. His sadness didn't look like an act.

Hanash tried a few different ways of getting at the timing of his trip, but his story didn't change. He returned to his desk chair and sat down, ignoring Abdel-Jalil. He pointed at Hamid, indicating he should continue.

"You said that you took the midnight bus to Fez," Hamid said, "but you and your friend went separate ways around eight. How did you spend those four hours before you traveled?"

"I went home and slept until eleven thirty, and then headed to the bus terminal."

"What was your relationship with Said like?"

"He was more than a brother to me, God rest his soul. We told each other everything, and didn't keep any secrets from one another."

Hanash lifted his head from the case file that he was pretending to read.

"No secrets, you say. So you knew all about the partying, drinking, sex, and other debauchery?"

"Sir, I follow my faith and carry out all of my religious obligations."

Hanash stood up, his blood boiling. "Did you kill your friend and the girl with him?" he shouted.

Abdel-Jalil was terrified, and his eyes widened. "You're accusing the wrong person, sir. I'm not a murderer!"

"Where did you hide the knife that you killed them with?"

"You're accusing the wrong person!"

Hanash pressed the button to open the door and the security guard appeared instantly.

"Take him to the basement so he can cool down a bit," he commanded.

Abdel-Jalil was in a state of shock. Hamid ordered him to put his hands up, and he took everything out of his pockets before the guard took him away.

"The most important thing is that we've got him," Hanash said. "We'll wait on a more comprehensive interrogation when we get the reports from the medical examiner and the forensics unit. But we need to look into his story. Call the police in Fez. Inform them about the nature of this crime and ask them to verify that Abdel-Jalil was with his family when he said he was. I want to know when he arrived and when he left."

After Hamid exited with his orders, Hanash picked up Abdel-Jalil's wallet and searched through it. Among a bunch of trivial things he found a bus ticket for Fez, for seat thirteen, with the date and time in question written on it.

12

At precisely ten o'clock, a waiter from the café next to the precinct brought Hanash his morning coffee. The moment he took a sip the phone rang. He looked at the number and saw it was the attorney general. He quickly put down the cup and lifted the receiver.

"Good morning, sir."

"Greetings, detective. The double murder—is there anything new?"

Detective Hanash sensed that the tone of his voice had changed, and he knew that he needed to deliver some reassuring news.

"We are awaiting the reports from the medical examiner and the forensics unit."

"Don't you have a strong lead or a suspect yet?" the attorney general interrupted.

"We have two suspects under temporary detainment. One is a close friend of the male victim. We've contacted the police in Fez to confirm that he really was there with his family, as he claims, at the time the murder took place."

"The other?"

"The other is a bouncer at the bar La Falaise, which the female suspect frequented. The bouncer has a strong alibi, confirming that he couldn't have been at the site of the crime when it happened."

"From what I remember the female victim was a prostitute, no?"

"Yes, that has been confirmed."

Detective Hanash could hear the attorney general's breathing down the phone.

"We need to take comprehensive measures regarding these clubs and bars for at least a week. I'm going to discuss this with the minister of the interior."

"As you wish, sir."

He put down the receiver and sat back in his chair. He hated when his superiors intervened in his work, except when it was to approve requests for extending the temporary detainment period. They didn't really know anything about police work, but they pretended to know everything. All they cared about was getting results as quickly as possible. If the case required making difficult decisions, they would always say the same thing: "Do whatever the circumstances demand." This was how they shirked any responsibility, leaving you to your fate.

He took a big gulp from the coffee cup, savoring it—it was excellent coffee and had a wonderful aroma. The security guard knocked on the door. Hanash opened it and the guard handed him the medical examiner's report.

The report from the medical examiner consisted of two pages, written in French and signed by the doctor who had carried out the autopsy. Hanash raced through the report, skimming over some of the routine language. What was most important was the time of death, and the report confirmed that it was between one and two in the morning. It also confirmed that the female victim was killed quickly, and that the two victims were surprised in bed and had engaged in anal sex. The murder weapon was confirmed to be a sharp blade, either a large knife or a sword. The report also detailed that, although Nezha had been disfigured, her body was not beaten like the male victim's had been. Said had been hit on the head and stabbed more than fifteen times. There was an attempt to cut off his penis but it seemed like the killer, or killers, gave up on this at the last minute. There were four lines in the report about the contents of the victims' stomachs—which were full of red wine and beer. The female victim had no food in her stomach.

Detective Hanash found himself immersed in thought after reading the report. The time of death was absolutely crucial, to be compared with the suspects' alibis. He reread the part detailing how the two were killed and started to feel more confident about his early theory that revenge was a motive. He picked up the phone to call the medical examiner.

"Good morning, professor. I read the report, but I have a question if you don't mind."

"Go ahead," the doctor responded, intimating that he was busy.

"Okay, thanks. Do you think the killer was a professional? Someone who knew how to use a knife?"

"No. No way," the doctor replied. "The stab wounds were totally random, and there wasn't resistance from the victims as they were likely killed in their sleep."

"Thank you very much," Hanash said, putting down the phone.

This medical examiner was extremely arrogant and dealt with police like they were beneath him. He would have to wait to see what the forensics report could tell him. Hopefully it would contain fingerprints that they could match to the murderer.

He started thinking about his men—what were Baba, Miqla, and Bu'u up to right now? He desperately needed Qazdabo snooping around to keep him in the loop.

There was a knock on the door and Hamid entered, looking despondent.

"Yes?" asked Hanash. "What is it?"

"Officer Azzadine called me from Fez. They interrogated Abdel-Jalil's family and confirmed that he really was there. His father met him around four thirty in the morning on Sunday, when he arrived at the bus station. He brought him home on his scooter. He left Fez today at four this morning in order to get back to Casablanca for his shift at eight."

The detective took out the bus ticket he had found in Abdel-Jalil's wallet and tossed it in the bin under his desk.

"Well, this ticket is useless." Then he remembered that Hamid wasn't aware he had the ticket. "That was the ticket for the bus he took to Fez. I found it in his wallet." He passed Hamid the medical report.

"What's everyone up to?" he asked, as Hamid read the report.

Hamid returned the report to his desk without comment. "Baba has just returned from the morgue with Said's father. I sent Bu'u to the neighborhood where the crime took place to sniff around a bit, see if he could find anything. Miqla is out looking for where they bought the alcohol."

Hanash nodded approvingly. "What are your first impressions of Said's father?" he asked.

"So far we haven't gotten a word out of him. He hasn't stopped crying. Do you want to see him?"

"If he doesn't have anything useful for the investigation, no need."

"We were able to ask if he had met Nezha, and if his son had problems with anyone. In both cases he answered no."

"Does he know his son's friend, Abdel-Jalil?"

"He never met him. Said's family is quite scattered. His parents are divorced, and we still haven't been able to track down his mother's address. His father doesn't know anything about his son's life. I don't think the murders had any connections to the relatives of the victims. We really need to find out who was in the room with them that night."

"The forensics report will be crucial in this regard."

Hanash hadn't even finished his sentence when there was another knock on the door. The guard gave him a file and left.

He looked through the forensics report excitedly, then tossed it to Hamid. Turning his back to the desk, he went to the window so he could look onto the streets, attempting to restrain his anger. Hamid read the forensics report and put it on the desk, astonished. The mood had quickly soured.

Hanash turned toward Hamid. "When you see the forensics team at the crime scene in their space suits, with all that fancy new equipment, you figure they'll work miracles! You see what they sent us? Absolutely nothing!"

"It says the fingerprints they found were partial and didn't allow them to determine anyone's identity," Hamid replied. "But it also says they could have been intentionally destroyed."

"I was waiting on this report to give us our prime suspect. It makes no sense that a third person who was with the victims didn't leave a single intact fingerprint on a wine bottle or cigarette butt."

Hanash threw himself on his chair, feeling hopeless. He skimmed the multipage report again. It was mainly filled with basic information that was not helpful at all.

"What now?" he wondered out loud.

Hamid didn't dare risk a response for fear that he'd say something that further stoked his boss's anger. But Hanash stared at him firmly, expecting a response.

"Isn't it possible that the murderer, or murderers, erased every trace of themselves, including their fingerprints?" Hamid said.

This comment made Hanash sink further into his chair. He looked out of sorts as he mulled this over.

"What we need is a new lead, a new angle," he said. "I have no interest, right now, in things that might take days or weeks to confirm. I don't need to remind you just how important the first forty-eight hours are in solving any crime."

Hamid nodded vigorously. "We'll shift into fifth gear, sir. We'll summon all the girls at La Falaise who knew Nezha. The murderer likely emerged from their circles. Like you said, 'Wherever alcohol and debauchery mingle, crime is just around the corner.' This should be taught at the police academy. This will be our guiding principle in this investigation instead of these useless reports."

Hanash started getting nervous as he listened to Hamid. If he encouraged him down this path, then the team would no doubt find out about Hotel Scheherazade, Hamadi, and the night he met Nezha.

"I can't believe that the papers printed what I said without attribution," he said, straightening up in his chair and changing the subject. "Listen, return to your office and look into what the others are doing. And what about the interrogation of Farqash and Abdel-Jalil? What's the latest there?"

Hamid got up and left.

Hanash felt a strange discomfort in his stomach, and looked at his coffee mug suspiciously. Then he called Naeema, to ask about the preparations for the celebration in Marrakesh that he promised to attend since he wasn't able to join them this morning.

His cell phone rang. It was Rubio. He told Hanash he'd read about the double murder that was all over the news. He asked him to come for lunch, and told him that he'd prepare his favorite table, but Hanash excused himself, promising to drop by again soon.

Hanash looked at his watch and saw it was twelve thirty. He rose, not sure what to do, and started collecting the various files and reports, unsure which came first or last. Before the medical and forensics reports arrived, he had been cautiously optimistic that he was close to getting his hands on something juicy. But optimism had given way to doubt and second-guessing. Had he started off on the wrong foot? It was hard to think of another direction he could have taken.

His hunger suddenly rendered him incapable of thought. He thought the best course of action was to make a quick trip home and have whatever Wafa had prepared. He put on his jacket and went into the bathroom to wash his hands. He looked in the mirror, straightened his tie, and headed out.

He stopped in the middle of the hallway as it dawned on him that he was leaving the office completely empty-handed, after hours of work. After having exhausted all his options, including the medical and forensics reports, he had no working theory and no meaningful evidence.

He returned to his office. Farqash and Abdel-Jalil both had alibis that checked out, so in a matter of hours their temporary detainment periods would be over. At that point he'd have an investigation file that was completely empty. He must leave no stone unturned, so he went back into his office and extracted Abdel-Jalil's bus ticket from the trash. He looked at it again and then reread the information carefully. He put it in his pocket and left his office quickly.

Detective Hanash raced through Casablanca's streets in one of the Japanese-model cars reserved for the highest-ranking officials. In less than fifteen minutes, he was at the entryway to Awlad Zayan bus terminal where he once again parked directly under a "No Parking" sign. This was another one of those assignments he would have entrusted to an officer under normal circumstances. He brought Abdel-Jalil's bus ticket to the employee at the Fez ticket booth.

"I need to authenticate this ticket," he said, in an authoritative tone.

The elderly employee behind the window looked up at him.

"If you are a policeman, sir, then I am at your service," he replied, with a hint of sarcasm.

"Head detective, criminal investigations."

The man stood up as straight as he could, given his crooked back, and opened the kiosk door. There was barely space for one person inside.

"At your service, sir. Please come in," he said, as he bowed his head respectfully.

The elderly employee motioned for the detective to take a seat on the one chair in the kiosk, while he remained standing. Hanash handed him the ticket.

"I need to verify whether the man who purchased this ticket in fact traveled to Fez on this bus."

The employee inspected the ticket and hesitated. "Yes, it's one of our tickets . . . Sunday, the midnight bus. Just a second, please."

He bent down so that his head nearly touched Hanash's belly. He opened a dirty drawer and extracted a folder that contained a bunch of timetables and started flipping through them.

"Sir, this folder"—he began explaining—"includes a list of all the buses that left the station since the beginning of the month. Here's the one for Sunday . . . midnight . . . seat thirteen."

"Did he travel or not?" asked Hanash impatiently.

"No, he didn't."

"Are you positive?"

"Look for yourself. Here you go," he said, passing the sheet to Hanash. "Before the buses pull out of the station a controller boards the bus to check everyone's tickets. On the sheet you're looking at, he checks the box with the seat number. Seat number thirteen is empty. There's no check. This means the person who bought the ticket didn't show up before the bus departed."

"Any chance he switched his seat for another?"

"That can only take place after the bus has left the station."

Hanash put the sheet in his pocket and got up hurriedly.

"I'm going to keep this as evidence."

Back in the car he took the sheet of paper from his pocket and looked it over again as if it were a precious document. Then he started laughing.

"That bastard is messing with us! He thinks we're fools."

He took out his cell phone before starting the engine and dialed Hamid's number.

"Have you had lunch?" he asked, his voice exultant.

"No. I'm still in the office with Said's father."

"You can leave that now. Go and get something to eat. Fill up—we need to be ready to work. I found something that might crack this case."

"Really? Okay, sir."

"I'll fill you in when I get back. But before you go, tell Kinko to put a piss-soaked rag in Abdel-Jalil's mouth to teach him a lesson about lying."

He hung up before Hamid had a chance to reply. Fifteen minutes later he was back downtown and stopped at Restaurant Jerome throughout on Harizi Street. The restaurant was owned by a Moroccan Jew and popular with the locals. It was one of the best-known restaurants in Casablanca, and its Muslim patrons far outnumbered its Jewish customers. Hanash beeped his horn and Jerome rushed out. He was a handsome man of around fifty. He had green eyes, a snub nose, and a large belly.

"Hello, detective," Jerome said in his Jewish-Moroccan accent. "What will it be?"

"Jerome, I see how busy it is, but if you could prepare some kidney sausage sandwiches for me, I'd be grateful."

Jerome opened his door for him. "Come on in. Better to eat inside."

"Ah, sorry, Jerome, I'm on an urgent case."

A look of concern spread over Jerome's face. "God protect us, what happened?"

"We received a warning that suicide bombers are going to blow themselves up in five minutes. Hurry up and make those sandwiches!"

Jerome laughed. "What is this? Scare tactics? I'm not leaving my country no matter what happens. There are explosions everywhere, no matter where you live."

In the five minutes it took Jerome to prepare the sandwiches Hanash sat in his car and reflected on the last terrorist blasts that had rocked Casablanca. It was all so incredibly absurd, he thought—these young men seeking any excuse to die, and finding that excuse through their embrace of a perverted extremist ideology.

Hanash found the hallways empty and all the office doors locked when he returned to the precinct. Even the security guard assigned to his office had gone to lunch.

He had everything he needed in his office—there were plates, knives, forks, glasses, and napkins. He prepared a table as if he were in a restaurant. When he opened the plastic bag from Jerome, he was surprised to find an entire meal, including salad and fruit. Before he could take his first bite the office phone rang. He reached out to pick up the receiver and immediately heard his wife's voice.

"Wafa told me that she prepared you something for lunch but you didn't go home."

"Yes," he lamented, "I forgot to tell her that I couldn't make it back today. An emergency came up at work. I'm eating sandwiches in my office at the moment. I'll tell her to leave the lunch for dinner."

He hung up and attacked Jerome's delicious sandwiches.

13

Two men lifted Abdel-Jalil by the armpits and moved him from Kinko's room in the basement to a holding cell. He couldn't walk on his own because the soles of his feet had been caned— they were split open and bloody. They tossed him into a corner of the cell, where he remained, crumpled on the ground and in anguish from his wounds, not to mention his hunger, thirst, and nausea from the urine-soaked rag that Kinko had stuffed in his mouth. Kinko was the best on the force when it came to intimidation and torture. He'd really honed his craft following the 2003 terrorist attacks in Casablanca. He regretted having to adapt to recent protocols, which demanded a bit more caution, such as not leaving discernible marks of torture.

Before the guards brought Abdel-Jalil into Hanash's office they let him wash his face and clean off his clothes, and they gave him a dry crust of bread with a bit of butter on it. They brought him up cuffed and pushed him into the center of the office. Hanash ordered the guard to remove his cuffs.

"Take a seat, Abdel-Jalil," he said in a paternal voice. "Now, take a good look at this sheet. Look closely at the box next to number thirteen, your seat number. Look closely . . . see how there is no mark next to number thirteen for the midnight bus to Fez on Sunday night? That means that you didn't go see your family."

Abdel-Jalil's face turned white and he couldn't look at Hanash.

"Lift up your head and answer the detective!" yelled Hamid.

"I swear to God I traveled. Ask my family in Fez."

Hanash circled around his desk and smacked the closet door.

"Now you've pissed off the boss," Hamid whispered, leaning into Abdel-Jalil. "Is that what you wanted?"

Hanash returned to his desk, his chest heaving. "Why did you force your family to lie?" he asked. "Do you know what will happen to them? All of them are going to be arrested for providing false information and misleading the police. I'm going to call the chief of police in Fez now and have them all arrested."

He lifted up the receiver and started entering the number.

"Your poor parents," Hamid added. "What did they ever have to do with this?"

Abdel-Jalil began sobbing and imploring Hanash not to make the call.

"I beg you, sir. My father has diabetes. This news would give him a heart attack."

Hanash put the phone down and glared at him. "Come on, Abdel-Jalil," he chided. "Be a man."

"Oh God, this is exactly what I feared," Abdel-Jalil said, as if he were addressing himself. "I'll tell you everything from the beginning."

He told them how he ran into Nezha after purchasing his bus ticket to Fez, and how he suggested that she join him at his friend's apartment, since he lived so close to the bus terminal. He mentioned that they agreed on three hundred dirhams for the night. When they arrived at Said's, Abdel-Jalil related, he was shocked to find Said already drunk when he opened the door, and said that Said immediately became infatuated with Nezha and wanted her for himself.

"I don't know how I got roped into drinking. Maybe it was because of my friend's behavior. He wanted Nezha for himself and was so aggressive in trying to kick me out of the place to be alone with her. I think every time he reminded me of my bus's departure time I drank more. Despite our friendship, I'm not his pimp! Did he really think I had hunted down a prostitute to bring back for him? Then he started asking me to go out to buy more cigarettes—to get rid of me. Then an idea came to me . . . well, more like the damn alcohol told me . . . why don't I head out, and when I get back and see that Said already had his way with Nezha, I'll have a turn myself, and get a bit of revenge by being rough. So I left the door slightly open and went out to the street, looking for someone selling cigarettes. I think I walked around for more than fifteen minutes until I found some. I know it was about that long because I smoked more than one on the way back. At that point, trust me, I wasn't thinking about Nezha nearly as much as I was thinking about Said. I remembered that his entire month's salary was in a drawer in his nightstand. I suddenly got scared that Nezha would steal his money. When I got back to the apartment I was surprised to find the door wide open. In the bedroom there was blood everywhere . . . it was still fresh. Steam was rising off it like when sheep are slaughtered at Eid. I couldn't believe my eyes. I wasn't sure if it was real or the alcohol was messing with me. Next thing I knew I was in the street, running. I desperately wanted to run into someone who I could tell, but at the same time I thought that what I saw might all have been an alcohol-induced hallucination. I kept running until I got home, despite the distance. I took a cold shower, and it was at that point I realized that there was no way that what I saw was some hallucination. The horrifying scene that I saw in my friend's bedroom was real. So what now? I thought. If I called the police . . . you guys . . . I'd immediately be a suspect, since I was the last one with Said and Nezha. I'd be detained until they could find the killer, in which case I'd lose my job. They'd have no sympathy at the factory—people are fired over anything. And then, even after you find the killer I'd have to give testimony about drinking and being involved with a prostitute, so I'd be imprisoned for those things anyway.

"So I was scared I'd be fired from my job if I called the police. I can't lose my job—I support my whole family. When

I saw the bus ticket in my wallet an idea came to mind. As I thought back through everything that happened, I was sure that no one had seen me, and no one else knew what happened. So why not just go to Fez as planned? I changed my clothes, went to the train station, and took the first train I could to Fez. That's the truth."

Hanash listened intently, and once Abdel-Jalil had finished he relaxed in his chair. Hamid, on the other hand, smiled sarcastically and shook his head, not believing a single word.

"You concocted this whole scenario just because you were afraid of losing your job?" Hamid said, ridiculing him. "Did you tell your family what happened?"

Abdel-Jalil seized up, and then he started bawling. "I told everyone what happened. My father said that the police are sophisticated and would solve the case in the blink of an eye. They were sure that the truth would come out and the killer would be apprehended yesterday. Then no one would even find out about the drinking and all the rest of it, and I wouldn't get fired."

Hanash reached his arms out over the desk as if he wanted to strangle Abdel-Jalil.

"Alcohol motivates lots of guys like you to commit crimes they would have never imagined. The booze intensified your jealousy. You lost it and killed them both."

"If you confess to the double murder," Hamid chimed in, "we'll look the other way regarding the drinking and debauchery charges, and you won't lose your job."

"Ha, right!" Hanash added. "But maybe it's best to confess to the drinking, since it's one of those defenses that could actually lessen your sentence in a murder trial."

Around three thirty, Detective Hanash gathered everyone in his office; the three officers were there, as well as Inspector Hamid. The officers were shooting the breeze before they got down to business. They were talking about Qazdabo, and how no one thought he was actually sick. They agreed that he was probably just desperate to see his wife, since they all knew how much he talked about women. Qazdabo didn't hide his frustration over the fact that he was by himself, sleeping in a damp office with rats, while the others got to return home to their wives. He also didn't really hide his role as the detective's informant. They all knew. But the others benefited from his tendency to play the double-agent role—he would warn his friends on the force if they were being monitored and update them about Detective Hanash's mood before they went to request something from him.

"Qazdabo will be in tomorrow," said Hanash, smiling, as he returned to his chair to start the meeting.

Hanash flipped through the interrogation files and other reports and then put the case file aside. He seemed to be brimming with a sense of satisfaction and resolve as he scanned the group of men sitting in front of him. He read the same emotions in their demeanors.

Hamid talked about the inspection of Abdel-Jalil's apartment, which hadn't uncovered anything of note. There was no trace of the murder weapon, or any bloodstained clothing. Hamid showed his boss a bunch of photos they had found in the apartment of Said and Abdel-Jalil together, photos taken at work and elsewhere, confirming their close friendship.

The only major decision they made during this meeting was to summon Abdel-Jalil's entire immediate family from Fez.

"I want them here tomorrow morning at eight," the detective ordered.

"We need to grill them," Hamid added, as he scribbled in his notebook. "We have to find out how involved they were in all this."

The prevailing mood in the office was that they were close to wrapping up this case, that they were closing in on victory. The real moment of glory would be when they reenacted the crime on site with a huge audience of television reporters, journalists, and photographers. Crime reenactments had started getting serious television coverage and the print media always plastered their front pages with headlines and photos from them. The reenactment was also when the lead investigators could speak directly to the media, and they would be portrayed as heroes.

Everyone in the office knew that Detective Hanash was dying to get to this closing ceremony, where he could declare in front of everyone gathered: "Wherever alcohol and debauchery mingle, crime is just around the corner."

The issue that still nagged everyone was the murder weapon. The report said it was either a large knife or a sword. Of late, thieves had actually been using swords during break-ins. Abdel-Jalil didn't have any priors, and certainly was not a thief, so how would he have gotten his hands on something like that? And how had he disposed of it? These issues were frustrating Detective Hanash. Dwelling on these uncertainties, he felt like he was falling into a black hole, so he would return again to the indisputable facts of the case.

Baba, the man who wheezed even when he wasn't exerting any physical effort, was the one who raised another issue the others had overlooked—the money that had disappeared from the crime scene. In Abdel-Jalil's confession they learned that he and Said had both received their wages that day. The first team on the scene had found an envelope with a pay stub from the factory for three thousand five hundred dirhams. According to Abdel-Jalil, Said had the money in an envelope in a drawer, but he denied having taken it after discovering the murders. Could the cash that disappeared be linked to the missing murder weapon?

No one in the office wanted to offer some half-baked hypothesis on this, fearing it would anger Hanash, but what if the motive behind the murder was theft, and not related to alcohol and sex?

"Could we follow up on the disappearance of this cash?" asked Bu'u.

"Abdel-Jalil put the cash in his pocket after taking his revenge," Miqla proposed, narrowing his eyes.

"If he was the one who stole the money, why did he tell us about it in the first place?" Baba shot back.

This question silenced them: it was a good point.

"Let's set aside for the moment the issue of the cash that disappeared," Hanash said. "The most important thing now is to figure out how to make this obstinate bastard confess where he hid the murder weapon."

Miqla's eyes lit up. "Let him spend a night with Kinko, hanging by his feet with that rag in his mouth," he suggested. "Tomorrow he'll confess that he even tried killing the pope himself!"

The officers laughed and Baba winked at Miqla knowingly. Whenever Miqla wanted to joke at Baba's expense he'd use this play on words, since the word *Baba* was also the name for the pope. These antics usually took place behind Hanash's back.

"Tell Kinko not to leave any marks," Hanash warned, agreeing to Miqla's suggestion.

"Kinko has modified his techniques according to the new human rights accord," joked Bu'u.

The meeting had lasted an hour and ten minutes and they all agreed on the same set of conclusions: Abdel-Jalil was the murderer; he had a strong motive, and he had contrived a story with his family to mislead the police. It was hard to see things any other way in spite of Abdel-Jalil's adamant denial or the issue of a missing murder weapon and cash.

Hanash remained in his office for a few more hours by himself, examining the documents, rereading the reports and interrogations, and trying to resolve some of the inconsistencies.

He felt as if there were loose ends, but he didn't know how to connect them to one another. What really incensed him was the total lack of useful evidence presented in the medical and forensics reports. If he wanted final confirmation of anything in these reports, he'd be waiting another couple of weeks at least.

He was the last to leave the precinct, at around seven. These two and a half extra hours were a gift he bestowed upon the administration. As he headed to his police car, his mood lightened. He was starting to get this feeling of being untouchable—a feeling he got only when he was close to solving a crime. And this crime had been giving him fits of anxiety because of his previous encounter with a victim. He smiled as he drove onto the wide avenue and pulled up in front of his daughter's salon.

The bright neon lights blinking in the salon window delighted him. He entered and found himself in heaven, surrounded by a cadre of beautiful young women. The oldest was no more than twenty-five. They were all dressed in the latest fashions, wearing outfits that exposed parts of their midriffs and lower backs. He quickly forgot what he had come for, and stood marveling at this exhibition of lovely, scented young bodies.

"We didn't expect to see you, sir. How can I help?" asked one his daughter's employees, who recognized that he was Manar's father.

He smiled bashfully, finding it difficult to put words together. "I'm here on Manar's behalf, since she's in Marrakesh. She asked me to check if you needed anything."

*

At eight o'clock sharp Hanash was in his office, clean-shaven and sharply dressed. He was wearing his Wednesday suit, a navy-blue Christian Dior that Rubio had given him as a gift last year. He had on a white button-down with a crimson tie. He called down to the café to order his morning coffee and then thumbed through the files on his desk, rereading a few important sections from the reports. He didn't even lift his eyes when the waiter entered to bring his coffee. He thanked him with a hand motion as he assiduously kept reading, searching for anything that might inspire him anew. Hamid arrived, and gave a salute before Hanash ordered him to sit.

As expected, Hamid was wearing a professionally pressed suit, although it was clear that he had bought it secondhand. The jacket had a stodgy British look to it, as if the previous owner was a lord in parliament. The necktie didn't quite match the suit's style.

"Has Qazdabo returned to work?" Hanash asked, smiling.

"Yes," Hamid replied, nodding. "He's in the office with the others."

"Okay, good. The first thing we're going to do today is hear out Abdel-Jalil's family."

Hamid nodded. "They're all here," he said. "They're in the hallway waiting. Would you prefer to interrogate them in my office?"

"Not before I take a look at them," Hanash said, pressing the button to open the door.

The whole family entered his office—Abdel-Jalil's two parents and three sisters, who were all veiled and attractive. The eldest was around forty, and the youngest was thirty-two. It was obvious that they had spent the night on the road. Their eyes were weary and bloodshot due to the approximately two hundred miles of travel that separated Fez and Casablanca. They all lined up next to one another in front of the detective. They made for a sad sight. Abdel-Jalil's mother looked completely distraught. Her face was white as a sheet, and she looked like she was carrying the weight of the world on her shoulders. His father was swaying and looked as though he might fall. The sisters stood with their heads bowed. They were all holding hands, as if they anticipated being separated into individual jail cells. Hanash looked at them in astonishment and exchanged a look with Hamid. He pressed the button again and ordered the guard to go get Abdel-Jalil.

"Why did you lie and force the rest of the family to lie?" Hanash asked the father.

In unison—as if they had rehearsed in advance—all five of them cringed and burst out in tears. Hanash saw how exhausted the parents were and ordered them to sit. He looked closely at the mother. She was thin but hardened, much tougher-looking than her frail husband. She wore a white jalabiya and her hair was drawn back behind a white headscarf. Her striking black eyes shifted between Hamid and Hanash.

"There is no way my son committed murder," she stammered. "I know my son. He is virtuous and tolerant, and has a

226

gentle heart. Since the day his father fell ill with diabetes he's become the breadwinner. Look at these women, sir. They are all stuck at home without jobs or husbands. Abdel-Jalil would prefer, a thousand times over, to be killed rather than abandon his sisters."

The sisters were sobbing by this point. The father's head drooped, rocking left and right.

"You haven't answered the detective's question," Hamid interrupted her sharply. "Why did you lie to the police when they interrogated you in Fez? You lied about the time of your son's arrival. You covered up his double murder."

"What you've done," interjected Hanash, "is punishable by law."

"We didn't lie, sir," said the father in a hoarse voice. "We told the police in Fez exactly what our son advised us to say. You have to understand, I'm more than seventy-five years old and I've worked with ceramics my whole life. We've always lived honorably, and we will die honorably, inshallah. What we did, sir, isn't lying, because we didn't accuse anyone, and we didn't offer false witness. We were in an impossible situation. My son is not a murderer. There is no way he could have killed someone. If he lied, it was for one reason: to keep his job."

There was a knock on the door. It opened, and Kinko pushed a handcuffed Abdel-Jalil into the center of the office. His face looked like death. He could barely stand on his bare feet. He tried to move toward his mother to embrace her, but instead collapsed on the ground in front of her.

"They're wrong . . . Mom, I've been wrongly accused," he said in a strained voice.

The office took on the atmosphere of a funeral, and it was impossible to continue with the interrogation.

As it approached eleven in the morning, after more than two hours of work, Hanash hadn't learned anything new. He entrusted Hamid with conducting the interrogations of the family members. The prime suspect, Abdel-Jalil, was now in a cell, still denying any involvement. Farqash had to be released from his temporary detainment. On top of everything, there was still no sign of the murder weapon or missing cash.

Hanash rocked back and forth in his chair, running through everything that had happened from start to finish. He had no idea who could have done it other than Abdel-Jalil. He was the last to see the two victims, and he had concocted a story, supposedly because he didn't want to lose his job. After seeing Abdel-Jalil's woeful family, was it not possible that he was also motivated to commit this heinous act because he wanted to steal Said's wages? The detective knew plenty of horrible murders had been committed for paltry sums, not exceeding a few dirhams. But the fact remained, Abdel-Jalil was the one who had told them about the cash. If he wasn't the thief, that meant someone else had entered the bedroom after he left, opened the nightstand drawer, and taken the cash, but left the pay stub in the envelope. Why hadn't the thief taken the envelope too? He made a connection as he rocked in the chair: the thief must not have known that the envelope had cash in it before he looked inside, or else he would have put the whole envelope into his pocket. He must have opened the envelope, looking for something to steal, come across the cash inside, taken it, and left the envelope in its place. Whoever the thief was had time to do all this before the police arrived. An image of the upstairs neighbor who had notified the police about the crime flashed into his mind. He searched feverishly among the reports until he found the interrogation file for the man. He reread it carefully and gave orders to Baba and Miqla to bring him back in.

Hanash got up to take a lap through the criminal investigations wing that he oversaw. He used a hand gesture to signal to everyone to continue working, and not stop to salute. But Qazdabo didn't comply—he stopped cold, as though he'd been struck by lightning, and gave an energetic salute. Hanash smiled and asked after his family, then continued on. When he approached Hamid's office he could hear the sisters wailing and the mother whimpering. He wondered how they would ever finish up the interrogation if they wouldn't stop crying.

Less than an hour later the man who had notified the police about the crime was standing in front of him. He could hardly compose himself, and was paralyzed by fear.

"Do you know why we brought you back here?" Hanash asked.

The man started crying like a bereaved mother and cursed himself for calling the police after discovering the crime scene.

Hanash ignored his wailing and accused him of stealing cash from an envelope in the drawer of the nightstand next to Said's bed. On top of that, he accused him of lying.

"We found your fingerprints on the envelope that had money stolen from it."

Hanash surprised even himself in saying this. He remained indifferent to the man who, by now, had fallen to his knees and was begging Hanash to let him go. Hanash thought he must be in denial over the accusations directed at him. He was fed up with him, so he called for Kinko. When he arrived, he gave him orders to deal with the man.

As usual when acting on an impulse, Hanash kept whatever was in his mind to himself, refusing to tell anyone until he found proof.

Hanash took the keys to Said's apartment out of a safe and snuck out of the office. He drove quickly to the crime scene and parked a few meters from the building.

As he opened the door, a nasty smell hit him and rats shot off in all directions. Everything in the apartment had remained untouched, just as they'd left it. When he flipped the light switch in the bedroom he was confronted by a disgusting scene—the blood all over the bed and walls had dried and tiny insects had begun feasting on these last human remains. He pinched his nostrils and opened the drawer in the nightstand. The envelope was still there with the paystub inside. He placed it in a plastic evidence bag and rushed back outside. He knew that while this envelope may not have held any importance during the initial investigation, it had become a crucial piece of evidence following Abdel-Jalil's confession about the cash that had vanished.

He drove immediately to the forensics lab. It was a small building, and looked nothing like the massive labs you saw on TV. He handed the envelope to the head of the forensics team and asked him graciously to deliver the results as soon as possible.

The results that the forensics team delivered were both unexpected and alarming. The only fingerprints on the envelope were those of Officer Qazdabo.

Hanash reread the report more than once, wondering how this could have happened without one of his men seeing Qazdabo. Hanash remembered his strange behavior before he left to see his family. This must be why he had claimed he was sick: it was because he had stolen the cash from the crime scene. There could be no doubt about it. Hanash recalled thefts by officers in previous cases, but never had this happened in a murder case that the whole nation was following.

A feeling of distress washed over him, and Hanash took a moment to calm down before he lifted the receiver and gravely summoned Hamid.

Hamid entered, his eyes wide with anticipation. He had expected the worst based on the tone of Hanash's voice. Hanash didn't even ask him to take a seat. He tossed the forensics report right at him, and Hamid started reading.

"This is horrible!" Hamid exclaimed hoarsely. "This is the end for Qazdabo. But, detective, we can't just accuse him based on these fingerprints. We have to get him to confess on his own."

Hanash got up and walked around his desk. "You're the one who was in charge of the investigation before I arrived!" he yelled. "Where were you when Qazdabo opened up the envelope and took the cash?" Hanash glared at Hamid.

"Detective," Hamid replied, trying to hide his refusal to assume responsibility. "Here's how it happened: we got a call from the man who discovered the crime—"

Hanash waved his hand, stopping him mid-sentence, and then picked up the phone to dial Kinko's number.

"Kinko, release the man who notified us of the crime immediately." He replaced the receiver and looked back at Hamid. "Continue."

"Like I was saying, sir, after I received the news from dispatch I gave orders to the security detail to head to the area, surround it, and guard the perimeter from looters or nosy bystanders. I didn't order Qazdabo to go with them, but when I arrived on the scene I found him inside, by himself. I was surprised to find him there, coming out of the bedroom pretending that he was about to throw up."

Hanash nodded, acknowledging the gravity of what he was hearing. He fell back into his chair, ordered Hamid to sit down, and picked up the phone to request Qazdabo.

"We need to coax him into talking about this without threatening him," Hanash said.

Qazdabo appeared at the office door and gave an anxious salute along with a silly smile.

"Please, come in and sit, Officer Qaddur," said Hanash, addressing him by his real name.

Qazdabo sat down half-heartedly. It was clear that he knew why he had been summoned.

"How is your family doing?" Hamid asked, smiling wryly.

"My eldest, Omar, who is fifteen, wants to drop out of school. He's really giving his mother a headache, and she's all alone with them while I'm up here."

Hanash handed him the forensics report. Qazdabo grabbed the paper and remained completely still as he looked it over. He returned it to Hanash and looked at him with his silly smile, indicating that he didn't quite understand what it said.

"What does this mean, sir?" Qazdabo asked.

Hanash tossed his head back lightly, trying to keep his composure. "Don't test me," he said, in a paternalistic tone. "Don't make your situation any worse. I'll give you one day to return the thirty-five hundred dirhams that you took. Then we'll clear all this from the records, and nothing will get out about it."

"I don't understand," said Qazdabo, in horror. "What are you talking about, sir?"

"On the day the investigation began," Hamid intervened, incensed, "I caught you coming out of the bedroom where the victims had been murdered. You were the first person to arrive at the scene. You took it upon yourself to enter the crime scene before I arrived!"

"Qazdabo, you don't want me to hand this forensics report over to another unit, do you?" Hanash asked. He reached out and grabbed the phone, waiting for Qazdabo's response.

Qazdabo lowered his head. He seemed to be weighing his options before giving a definitive response. Finally he lifted his head, his eyes welling up with tears.

"Will you be able to forgive me, sir?" he said imploringly. "Could you at least show mercy for my children, who would become homeless?"

"Confess to what happened first!" Hamid rebuked him with unexpected severity.

"I give you my word," said Hanash.

"Okay, I'll confess." Qazdabo closed his eyes, placed his quivering hands on his knees, and began his confession. "Yes, I was the first to arrive at the crime scene. It must have been the devil himself who tempted me to look in the open night-stand drawer. Then I found the envelope and saw the money. I said to myself: 'The rightful owner of this money has been murdered, and left us for eternity.' Meanwhile, I'm here on earth drowning in debts. I send all my wages to my wife in Taza, and you know I have five children. You know I can't even rent a room here in the city. You're the one who allows me to use the abandoned office on the top floor."

While confessing, Qazdabo hadn't been paying attention as Hanash got up from his chair, hung his jacket on the coat hanger, and rolled up his sleeves. Hanash smacked Qazdabo so forcefully that he flew out of the chair.

"You bastard!"

Hanash had never felt so enraged before. Even in Tangier, when he was working with drug traffickers and violent criminals, he had never been as angry and disappointed as he was now. He felt like Qazdabo was mocking him and had completely underestimated the consequences. Even worse, he couldn't believe that Qazdabo thought that his personal circumstances might save him. Qazdabo crawled over to Hanash and fell at his feet, kissing them in a gross display of humiliation.

"The fate of my children is in your hands. Please don't send me to prison. You gave me your word, sir. I didn't find 3,500 dirhams in the envelope; I found 3,200."

Instead of making things better, this further enraged Hanash, and he kicked Qazdabo in the stomach.

"You don't deserve any mercy!" he shouted indignantly. "You're a corrupt piece of shit who gives our profession a bad name!"

Up until that moment, Qazdabo had been expecting forgiveness, but when he saw the detective reach for the phone to call for the security guards he drew the gun out of the holster under his armpit, aimed it at Hanash's heart, and fired. The phone fell from Hanash's hand, and he crashed to the floor. Before Hamid had a chance to react, Qazdabo put the gun in his mouth and pulled the trigger. The bullet passed right through his skull and lodged itself in the wall, along with shards of bone and pieces of brain.

14

THE ATTORNEY GENERAL'S OFFICE CHOSE to carry out the reenactment of the crime while Detective Hanash was still in the hospital, recovering from the gunshot wound, which, thankfully, had just missed his heart. All media outlets were invited to attend, and television crews reported live from the scene. At ten o'clock in the morning a police van pulled up with Abdel-Jalil handcuffed inside, surrounded by four muscular police officers. The crowd was so large that all the roads leading up to the crime scene were barricaded, and traffic in surrounding areas came to a standstill. When Abdel-Jalil was taken out of the vehicle, shrieks and jeers rang out from the crowd, demanding his public execution.

Hamid, who had been with Hanash every step of the way, oversaw the reenactment of the crime. He was surrounded by the nation's top security officials, all dressed in black suits with dark sunglasses. Despite the incredible satisfaction that accompanied solving a double murder of this caliber, the officials who gave television interviews did not present themselves as the heroes in some crime drama, as usually happened. Instead, they showered their bedridden colleague Detective Hanash with praise, and gave him all the credit for solving the crime.

A male and a female officer played the roles of the victims during the reenactment. They stretched out on the bed and a white sheet was placed over them. They asked Abdel-Jalil, who seemed completely bewildered, to reenact how he had murdered the victims. Baba provided him with a plastic sword, just like the ones children play with. In front of all the cameras, Abdel-Jalil yielded to his orders and began swinging the plastic sword down on the victims. The whole thing didn't last more than five minutes. Hamid intervened twice to demand that Abdel-Jalil deliver a more realistic reenactment of the murder. It was obvious that Abdel-Jalil was putting on a poor performance, simply trying to do what he was told.

Eight months later Abdel-Jalil was sentenced to be executed, despite having denied throughout the trial that he had committed the double murder. A confession had been extracted in a police interrogation room, though. The prosecution's case was based on several pieces of evidence. Among them were the bus ticket that was never used, the bus register that confirmed he hadn't traveled on the midnight bus, and the fact that he was the last person confirmed to have been with the victims. The prosecution established his motive to commit murder and relied also on the interrogations of Abdel-Jalil's family, who all confessed to lying. It was true that the murder weapon had still not been found, and the suspect denied all charges, but this did not prevent the court from convicting him and sentencing him to death.

Ruqiya didn't get the chance to attend the trial. She died from a heart attack only a month after her daughter was murdered. One morning, she hadn't woken as usual to perform the dawn prayers, and when Ibrahim tried to wake her he found her body stiff. Her eyes were open, and she looked like she'd greeted death kindly. Ibrahim considered his mother's parting a relief from the torturous kidney pain she had been suffering.

Three days after his mother's burial, Ibrahim vanished into thin air. No one knew where he went. Everyone in Kandahar assumed that he had headed to Tangier to attempt an illegal crossing into Spain.

The only Kandahar resident who attended the trial was the neighborhood muezzin, Driss. He had become the undisputed leader of Kandahar after Sufyan left for Syria. Driss had started preaching, and on the eve of the trial gave a sermon in the neighborhood mosque about how immorality tore apart families that had once been unified. He developed a unique charisma that attracted older residents of the neighborhood as well, even though he was only twenty-one years old. There was something about his thick beard, Afghani clothes, determined walk, and the fervent determination in his eyes that made him both feared and loved, especially by the girls in the neighborhood. He convinced many young girls to put on the full niqab, instead of just the veil. When he made public his intention to marry, nearly every eligible girl in the neighborhood came forward. He chose the most beautiful among them: the chicken seller's daughter. She was a chemistry student at the technical college, and one of the first who had put on the niqab out of love and devotion to his message.

Driss also got Salwa to close her salon. She acceded to his request without putting up a fight, and begged for his forgiveness.

Driss was provided with a respectable monthly income by the merchants in the neighborhood market. He used some of the money to rent the area adjacent to the mosque, which was reserved for selling medicinal herbal cures, as well as religious books and cassettes.

Driss launched a venture called Prepared Islamic Foods, on the suggestion of his brother-in-law, who also sold chicken. He and his followers sold cheap and delicious meals composed of onion with chicken innards, as well as minced, spiced sardines. They had wheeled carts to move about the neighborhood. The venture became quite successful, and the local youth who followed Driss would work all day, and share their profits every evening.

One night, around ten thirty, Driss received a phone call from Syria. The voice was choppy and distorted, and the line cut out completely more than three times. Sufyan's voice had changed, taking on a Levantine inflection. He spoke in short, concise sentences, as if he had received orders about what to say. Sufyan asked how his father was doing, and told

Driss to send him his regards. Sufyan said that he couldn't speak to his father directly, since he was hard of hearing. Then he asked about Ibrahim and the neighborhood. The line dropped again. Sufyan called back and resumed speaking in a terse official tone, as if reading an announcement. He said: "Salam Alaykum, I'm in Syria and I'll be carrying out a martyrdom mission tomorrow in the name of God. I request forgiveness by all . . ."

The newscasts reported the massive blast that shook a popular marketplace in Syria, resulting in the death of twenty individuals, with hundreds more injured. On the very same day, someone who called himself Abdel-Qahar called Driss and succinctly informed him of Sufyan's death.

The phone calls that Driss received had been intercepted by the Moroccan intelligence services, who eavesdropped on all communication coming from Syria. Driss was at the neighborhood mosque getting ready to deliver the afternoon call to prayer when they snatched him and brought him into custody. Three masked men brought him to a secret facility. They treated him well at first, since he cooperated and told them everything about his relationship with Sufyan. He said that Sufyan had been the leader in organizing the proselytization and dispatch of Moroccan fighters to Iraq and Syria. Driss revealed even more information when the interrogators decided to hang him upside down and apply electric shocks to his genitals. The interrogators were stunned when he confessed that Sufyan had murdered two people before he left Morocco.

After extracting these confessions, a special unit was dispatched to Sufyan's family home. They found a long sword wrapped in newspaper hidden in a trashcan on the roof of the house.

The laboratory analysis verified that the dried blood on the sword was, in fact, that of Nezha and Said.

Driss denied any involvement in the murders, but he did confess that his friend Sufyan had been infatuated with Nezha since he was fifteen years old. He used to send her love letters, and wanted to marry her. But Nezha slipped from his grasp after her father's passing, and she spiraled downward. Sufyan used to follow her everywhere, without her knowing, and he knew her every move. Sufyan had tried to forget about her, but couldn't. Driss concluded: "Before Sufyan traveled to Syria, he said that an angel had come to him in a dream and ordered him to cleanse the neighborhood of its impurities."

Selected Hoopoe Titles

Whitefly
by Abdelilah Hamdouchi, translated by Jonathan Smolin

The Final Bet
by Abdelilah Hamdouchi, translated by Jonathan Smolin

A Beautiful White Cat Walks with Me
by Youssef Fadel, translated by Alexander E. Elinson

hoopoe is an imprint for engaged, open-minded readers hungry for outstanding fiction that challenges headlines, re-imagines histories, and celebrates original storytelling. Through elegant paperback and digital editions, **hoopoe** champions bold, contemporary writers from across the Middle East alongside some of the finest, groundbreaking authors of earlier generations.

At hoopoefiction.com, curious and adventurous readers from around the world will find new writing, interviews, and criticism from our authors, translators, and editors.